英語聽&說

中級篇

白野伊津夫
Lisa A. Stefani　著

沈薇　譯

CD
BOOK

LISTENING & SPEAKING
STRATEGIES
INTERMEDIATE COURSE

三民書局

前　言

　　本書是《英語聽＆說》系列繼「入門篇」、「初級篇」之後，隆重推出的「中級篇」。「中級篇」的編排是以學完「入門篇」、「初級篇」的讀者，或是已經在聽與說的方面具有基礎會話能力的學習者為對象。希望本書能幫助各位聽懂日常生活中或商業環境中英語的自然會話方式，並同時達成開口說流利英語的目的。

　　我們之所以規劃本系列書，是依據「會話應該從聽開始」這種逆向思考的基本理念。許多劃時代的變革或是偉大的發明都是由與眾不同的逆向思考所帶來的成果，關於這點當然不用在此多加說明。在日常生活中，我們也因逆向思考而受惠良多。例如：在文件及資料的整理方面，日本百萬暢銷作品《「超」整理法——資料檢索與概念的新系統》的作者野口悠紀雄先生便顛覆了「整理＝分類」這樣的一般想法，主張以「時間」為主軸的「不需分類的整理法」。這本書的大賣也正清楚地告訴我們，必定有許多人因為這種不同凡「想」的整理方式而大幅減少了花在整理書房、管理文件資料上的時間及精神，而我也是受惠者之一。

　　逆向思考也能在英語的學習上帶來良好的效果。傳統的學習方式是「從說開始」，注重完整背誦某一情境下可能派得上用場的會話句子。但有經驗的人都知道，一旦要用英語應對實際狀況時，卻往往說不出記在腦海裡的句子。不論多麼用功地反覆背誦，英語會話就是沒有明顯的進步，原因在於這種方法正違背人類學習語言的自然過程。若想將英語說得很溜，就應該像小孩學習母親講話一樣——「從聽開始」。異國婚姻下或海外歸國的小孩，其第二外語的能力之所以比較好，就是長期在聽的環境下學習語言的緣故；他們或是跟隨父母親，或是從與當地的小孩一起遊玩

讀書的過程中培養聽力。聽力與口語表達能力有著密不可分的關係，聽力若提升，口語表達能力必定也能大幅度地進步。

　　但到了大人的階段，往往容易因無法理解對方所說的話而感到不安與害怕，這一點正是造成英語會話能力進步的障礙。不管對方說什麼，皆回答 Yes 或傻笑地當場敷衍過去，這將會產生受挫的心理，不僅無心期待下一次的對話，還會刻意避開任何與外國人輕鬆閒聊的機會。相反地，當培養並提升聽力後，在與外國人士對話時，就能接收 (input) 對方所說的話語，記在腦海裡；以後遇到適當的時機，就能化作自己的話語傳送 (output) 出去。而且，有良好的聽力可以聽懂電視及廣播電台的即時資訊，也能簡單順利地將聽到的內容融入於日常會話之中。尤其在與多數外國人同時對談的場合中，更需具備良好的聽力，若無法理解正常速度下的英文，就無法順利進行溝通。

　　衷心希望「英語會話從聽開始」這一座右銘可以激勵各位精進學習，無論在日常生活中或商場上都能廣泛靈活運用英語。

　　最後，謹向經常給予建議及鼓勵的研究社出版部佐藤淳先生，以及協助完成本書的鈴井加奈子小姐，致上感謝之意。

白野伊津夫
Lisa A. Stefani

目 次

前言
本書使用方法

本書共十五章，各章分 **Listening** 及 **Speaking** 兩大部分。Listening 的部分有四個小單元，Speaking 的部分則由五個小單元組成。

Listening

首先出現的「**Warm-up/Pre-questions**」是測驗在聽完各章主題下的英文短文後，能聽懂多少內容的選擇題。請聽完 CD 播放一次後立即作答。正確作答的要訣在於注意聆聽內容中涵蓋的重要訊息。由於是聽力的熱身運動，所以可以輕鬆面對。

會話的聽力練習則分成三個步驟，讓學習者循序漸進檢驗自己對內容的理解度。「**Listening Step 1**」是透過選擇題，練習粗略抓住初次聽到的會話內容概要。請聽完 CD 播放一次後立即作答。只要理解會話的大概內容，順著會話的進展，就能獲得正確的解答，不需在意細節，掌握內容的要點即可。

「**Listening Step 2**」是練習正確聽懂會話中涵蓋的重要訊息。首先要自我檢測是否能完全了解會話中出現的關鍵字意義，再開始做聽力的填空練習，以練習正確聽出句子中的特定單字。之後，再聽一次會話並回答兩個問題。聽力秘訣在於掌握 5W1H 中的 who, what, when, where 的要點。

「**Listening Step 3**」是培養完全聽懂會話內容的能力，以及練習判斷會話主角行為的原因和預測將來會如何發展。首先，先自我檢測是否理解會話中出現的片語和重要語句的意義，緊接著做聽力的填空練習，幫助聽懂之前出現過的片語和重要語句。最後，再聽一次會話並回答三個問題。正確解題技巧在於將焦點擺在 5W1H 中的 why 和 how 作答。

Speaking

　　此部分的「**會話**」(dialog) 可說是該章的重點, 介紹該章的主題內容。首先, 請先默念會話內容理解意思, 若有不懂的地方再看「中譯」或「語法」說明。接下來聽 CD, 充分掌握英語的發音、節奏及語調後再發出聲音朗讀。朗讀時, 最好是將自己融入為會話主角, 並確認自己的英語是否與 CD 播放的英語一樣流暢。建議可以採取聽 CD 後朗誦、朗誦後聽 CD 的間歇式 (interval) 練習法學習。若對發音有自信, 也可以採用投影練習法 (shadow training), 這是緊跟著 CD 馬上覆誦的有效學習法。練習完之後, 可以切掉開關, 試著一個人大聲唸, 看看自己的發音是否接近 CD 中外國人的腔調。相信經過這一連串的練習, 至少可誦唸 20 到 30 次的會話, 結果必能幫助脫口說出自然流利的英語。

　　「**Speaking Function**」中會提供不同的說法來表達相同的意思。例如: 要向對方表示「我確信」時, 常會以英文 I'm sure... 或 I'm certain... 等說法來表示, 其實還可以說成 I'm positive... / I'm confident... / I bet... / I have no doubt... 等其他的替換句。至於這些相似句的用法及其在語感上有什麼不同, 可以參照「解說」中的說明。請務必仔細聽 CD, 做好後續練習的準備。

　　「**代換、角色扮演**」是練習流利說出在「Speaking Function」中學得的各種替換句。首先, 「代換」練習是邊看 Function 的基本句, 邊聽 CD 再大聲唸出代換詞句的部分, 請反覆練習直到可以順口說出 Function 的英語句子來。「角色扮演」是視 CD 為談話對象的練習, 先注意聆聽完整的對話示範, 然後當聽到嗶一聲後即說出適切的英語對應。剛開始可以看書說, 但希望經過幾次練習後能不用看書而立即回答。

　　「**覆誦重要語句**」的單元是希望學習者再度熟習會話中出現的重要用語。在清楚了解重要用語的意義之後, 聆聽 CD 並緊跟其後大

聲唸出英文句子來。請反覆練習直到可以流利說出。

　　最後的「**實力測驗**」則是提供某一情境，讓學習者自我檢驗是否能就該章所學說出流利的應用語句對應。若是能立即回答三種不同的說法，即是及格，可以證明自己有不錯的學習能力。

Listening

Warm-up / Pre-questions

 請聽《Track 1》的氣象預報後回答下面問題。

週末會是怎樣的天氣?
  (A) 下大雨
  (B) 陣雨
  (C) 晴時多雲

內容　Sudden showers expected through the weekend, clearing by Tuesday.

中譯　預測本週末是陣雨的天氣, 至少要到下週二之後才會放晴。

解答　(B)

解說　廣播或電視在播報氣象時, 經常使用簡略的說法。上述的完整句子為 Sudden showers are expected through the weekend and it will be clearing by Tuesday.。其中, sudden showers 為「短暫陣雨」、clear 為「放晴」之意。

Listening Step 1

 請聽《Track 2》的會話後回答下面問題。

會話中的兩位女士在談論什麼話題？
(A) 去野餐要穿的衣服
(B) 去野餐要帶的食物
(C) 野餐的地點

解答　　　　　　　　　　　　　　　　　　　　　　　(B)

Listening Step 2

熟悉下列關鍵字

company picnic　公司野餐
spicy chicken wings　辣雞翅
sound　聽起來；似乎
bet　打賭（肯定之意）
true　真實的
sign-up list　簽名單
dish　（深底的）大盤子
potato salad　馬鈴薯沙拉
plate　（淺的）盤子
hot wings (=spicy chicken wings)　辣雞翅
awful　糟糕的，極壞的
post　公佈；公告
sign-up sheet　簽名用紙
one-day notice　一日的通知
worth　值得～的
canopy　天篷（遮雨、遮陽用的簡單帳棚）
lately　最近
unpredictable weather　無法預料的天氣

1 請聽《Track 3》並在括弧內填入正確答案。

1. I was thinking of spicy (　　　) wings.
2. Yes, but I (　　　) at least five other people have the same idea.
3. Maybe we can (　　　) a sign-up sheet tomorrow.
4. That is only one-day (　　　).
5. Maybe we should have people sign up to bring (　　　) also.

解答

1. I was thinking of spicy (chicken) wings.
2. Yes, but I (bet) at least five other people have the same idea.
3. Maybe we can (post) a sign-up sheet tomorrow.
4. That is only one-day (notice).
5. Maybe we should have people sign up to bring (canopies) also.

1 請再聽一次《Track 2》的會話後回答下面問題。

1. 野餐活動何時舉辦?
   (A) 星期五
   (B) 星期六
   (C) 星期日

2. 會話裡其中一人提出了什麼建議?
   (A) 張貼個人會攜帶前往的食物登記表
   (B) 分配好哪些人帶什麼食物
   (C) 製作聯絡電話表

解答　　　　　　　　　　　　　　　　　1. (B)　　2. (A)

Listening Step 3

熟悉下列語句

I'm really not sure.　我實在不太確定。
think of　考慮～（的事）
That sounds good.　那聽起來不錯。
That could be true.　那有可能。
end up with　最後以～為結束
That would be awful!　那實在是太糟糕了!
fill out　填寫（表格）
It's worth a try.　那值得一試。
we better not do　我們最好不要做
take chances with　冒險，碰運氣

1 請聽《Track 4》並在括弧內填入正確答案。

1. That could (　　　) (　　　).
2. We might (　　　) (　　　) (　　　) 8 dishes of potato salad and 5 plates of hot wings!
3. Do you think people will (　　　) (　　　) (　　　)?
4. It's (　　　) (　　　) (　　　).
5. We better not (　　　) (　　　) (　　　) with this unpredictable weather.

解答
1. That could (be) (true).
2. We might (end) (up) (with) 8 dishes of potato salad and 5 plates of hot wings!
3. Do you think people will (fill) (it) (out)?
4. It's (worth) (a) (try).

5. We better not (take) (any) (chances) with this unpredictable weather.

 請再聽一次《Track 2》的會話後回答下面問題。

1. Amy 在擔心什麼？
   (A) 可能無法參加野餐活動
   (B) 不會做美味的食物
   (C) 或許有許多人會帶相同的菜色前往

2. Amy 對於張貼登記表一事有何想法？
   (A) 張貼的時間太短了
   (B) 現在貼已經太遲了
   (C) 張貼在哪裡是個問題

3. Amy 為什麼提出也應該對能攜帶雨棚前往的人做張登記表？
   (A) 因為太陽很大，需要利用雨棚遮陽
   (B) 因為要讓小朋友盡興遊玩
   (C) 因為或許會突然下雨也說不定

解答   1. (C)   2. (A)   3. (C)

Speaking

會話

 請再聽一次《Track 2》。

Beth: What are you bringing to the company picnic this weekend,
Amy?

Amy: I'm really not sure. I was thinking of spicy chicken wings.

Beth: That sounds good.

Amy: Yes, but I bet at least five other people have the same idea.

Beth: That could be true. We should have made a sign-up list so we would know who was bringing what.

Amy: I know. We might end up with 8 dishes of potato salad and 5 plates of hot wings!

Beth: That would be awful! Maybe we can post a sign-up sheet tomorrow. The picnic is not until Saturday.

Amy: That is only one-day notice. Do you think people will fill it out?

Beth: It's worth a try. I think it will make the picnic more enjoyable.

Amy: All right. Let's do it. Maybe we should have people sign up to bring canopies also.

Beth: That is a good idea. It has been raining a lot lately.

Amy: Yes, we better not take any chances with this unpredictable weather.

中　譯 ···

貝絲：艾美，妳打算帶什麼菜來參加這個週末舉行的公司野餐？

艾美：我還沒拿定主意，不過我在考慮要帶辣雞翅。

貝絲：辣雞翅不錯。

艾美：是啊，不過我敢打賭至少會有五個人跟我有同樣的想法。

貝絲：有可能喔。其實我們應該製作一張簽名表以確定誰會帶什麼菜色來才對。

艾美：是啊，否則最後可能會變成八個人帶馬鈴薯沙拉、五個人

帶辣雞翅。

貝絲：那就糟了。野餐要到星期六才舉行，或許我們應該明天就
　　　將簽名表張貼出來。

艾美：不過也只剩一天來通知大家了。妳認為大家會填嗎?

貝絲：至少可以試一試。這麼一來才能讓野餐玩得更盡興。

艾美：好吧，我們就這麼辦。或許我們也應該確認會有人帶雨棚
　　　來。

貝絲：最近天氣經常下雨，這是個好主意!

艾美：對啊，天氣難以預測，我們最好要事先準備好。

語 法

● should have + 過去分詞

假設語氣的句型，表示「應該做～（但沒做）」。

We *should have made* a sign-up list so we would know who was bringing what. (其實我們應該製作一張簽名表以確定誰會帶什麼菜色來才對。)

● have + 受詞 + 不定詞原形

have 作使役動詞，表示「使～做…」之意。

Maybe we should *have people sign up* to bring canopies also.
(或許我們也應該確認會有人帶雨棚來。)

I'll *have Tom wash* my car. (我要湯姆幫我洗車。)

● have/has been + 現在分詞

以現在完成進行式表示「一直做著～」。

It *has been raining* a lot lately. (最近一直下雨。)

● better not + 動詞

原為「had better not + 動詞」的用法，但 had 在口語中常省略。

We *better not take* any chances. (我們不要冒險比較好。)

Speaking Function 1

請聽《Track 5》。

1. A: Do you think he will come to the picnic?

   B: I'm sure he will.

2. A: I wonder why he hasn't come yet.

   B: I bet he has forgotten the picnic.

3. A: What are you bringing to the picnic?

   B: I'm not really sure.

解說

● 表示對事物的確信，可以使用 I'm sure... 或 I'm certain... 這兩種基本的說法。若要表示「他一定會成功」，可以說 I'm sure he will succeed. 或 I'm certain he will succeed.。sure 和 certain 的不同在於：sure 原則上是經過個人主觀判斷之後的確信；相對地，certain 的確信則是因擁有確切的證據或根據。我們也可以用 quite, really, absolutely, fairly 等副詞來強調確信的程度，例如：I'm quite/really/absolutely/fairly sure he will come.。此外，確信的說法還有 I'm positive.../ I swear.../ I'm confident.../ I have no doubt.../ I bet... 等，這些都是表示強烈的確信。

● 並不確信時，可以用否定句的形式表達，如 I'm not sure/certain that's a good idea.。也可以添加 what 或 whether 等疑問詞或連接詞造句，如 I'm not sure what to do.（我不確定該怎麼做）或 I'm not sure whether he will agree or not.（我不確定他是否會同意）。

練習 1 【代換】

請隨《Track 6》做代換練習。

1. *I'm sure*   he'll agree with us.

> I'm quite sure
> I'm absolutely sure
> I'm certain
> I'm positive
> I'm confident
> I bet
> I have no doubt

2. I'm not really sure *what to bring*.

> what to say.
> how much it is.
> where to park the car.
> when I should come.
> why he said that.
> whether I should stay or not.

練習 2【角色扮演】

 請隨《Track 7》在嗶一聲後唸出灰色部分的句子。

1. A: Do you think you can finish the report by Wednesday?
   B: I'm sure I can.

2. A: I don't think he can finish the report by Thursday.
   B: I bet he can.

3. A: What are you bringing to the party?
   B: I'm not really sure.

練習 3【覆誦重要語句】

① 請隨《Track 8》覆誦英文句子。

1. think of 「考慮～（的事）」
   ↳ I'm thinking of something else.（我在考慮其他的事。）

2. sound 「聽起來；似乎」
   ↳ That sounds good.（那聽起來不錯。）

3. could be true 「有可能是真的」
   ↳ That could be true.（那可能是真的。）

4. end up with 「最後以～為結束」
   ↳ We might end up with six people.
   （我們最後可能剩下六個人。）

5. awful 「糟糕的，極壞的」
   ↳ That would be awful!（那樣實在是太糟了。）

6. not ～ until... 「還沒～直到…」
   ↳ The store does not open until 9 o'clock.
   （這家商店要到九點以後才會營業。）

7. fill out 「填寫（表格）」
   ↳ Will you fill out the application form?
   （能否請你填寫這張申請表格?）

8. worth a try 「值得嘗試」
   ↳ It's worth a try.（這件事值得一試。）

9. have + 人 + 原形不定詞 「使人做～」
   ↳ I'll have Tom meet you at the airport.
   （我會叫湯姆去機場接你。）

10. have/has + been + 現在分詞 「一直做著～」
    ↳ It has been raining a lot lately.（最近經常下雨。）

實力測驗

擔任司機的你正開車送要去海外出差的經理到機場，但是車子塞在半路上，無法以正常的速度前進，經理一副緊張的表情問你 "Do you think I can make my flight?"（你想我能搭上飛機嗎?），你看了一下錶，確定離報到的時間還十分充裕。請練習以三種不同的說法告訴他「我確定您一定能搭上」。

參考解答

1. I'm sure you can make it.
2. I'm quite positive you can make it.
3. I'm confident you can make it.

Chapter 2

A Job Interview 求職面試

Listening

Warm-up / Pre-questions

 請聽《Track 9》的求才廣告後回答下面問題。

這家公司正在徵求什麼人才？
(A) 電腦技術人員
(B) 電腦製圖人員
(C) 電腦排版人員

內容　Cerritos Corporation is now accepting applications for 3 computer technician positions. Must be qualified in both PCs and Macs. If interested, please e-mail your resume to: Jdavis@cerritos.com.

中譯　西利多公司目前誠徵三位電腦技術師。條件為必須熟悉個人電腦與麥金塔電腦。意者請將履歷以電子郵件的方式寄至 Jdavis@cerritos.com。

解答　(A)

解說　求才等廣告若因前後關係使得主詞非常明確時，通常會省略主詞。例如 Must be qualified in both PCs and Macs. 句中便省略了主詞 All the applicants。此外，accept 為「受理」、computer technician 為「電腦技術人員」、position 為「職位」、qualified 為「有資格的」、PCs 為「一般個人電腦」、Macs 為「使用蘋果公司麥金塔系統的電腦」、e-mail 為「發送電子郵件」、resume 則是「履歷表」之意。

Listening Step 1

 請聽《Track 10》的會話後回答下面問題。

Jason 現在在做什麼?

　(A) 面試求職者

　(B) 進行採訪

　(C) 接受面試

解答　　　　　　　　　　　　　　　　　　　　　　　(C)

Listening Step 2

熟悉下列關鍵字

complete　完成

technician　技術人員

certification course　資格課程

bachelor's degree　學士學位

currently　目前, 現在

position　職位

responsibility　責任

allow　允許, 許可

latest technology　最新科技

co-worker　同事

closely　緊密地; 親密地

efficiently　有效率地

deadline　截止日期, 最後期限

impressive　令人印象深刻的

specifically　特別地

growth　成長; 進步

```
starting salary    起薪
workday    工作日
typical    典型的
issue    問題
reputation    名聲，信譽
employee    職員
```

1 請聽《Track 11》並在括弧內填入正確答案。

1. Where do you (   ) work?

2. I'm a (   ) for Garrett Technologies.

3. Why do you want to work for our company (   )?

4. Our workdays are a bit longer than the (   ) workday.

5. Your company has a great (   ) for taking care of its employees.

解答

1. Where do you (currently) work?

2. I'm a (technician) for Garrett Technologies.

3. Why do you want to work for our company (specifically)?

4. Our workdays are a bit longer than the (typical) workday.

5. Your company has a great (reputation) for taking care of its employees.

1 請再聽一次《Track 10》的會話後回答下面問題。

1. Jason 是個怎樣的人？

 (A) 大學時代才開始學會電腦的人

 (B) 擁有碩士學位

 (C) 從小就開始使用電腦

2. Jason 現在在哪裡工作?

   (A) Garrett Technologies 公司

   (B) Cerritos 公司

   (C) 在家工作

解答   1. (C)   2. (A)

Listening Step 3

熟悉下列語句

about yourself   關於你自己
my whole life   我這一生(指生命中所有的時間)
in addition to   此外;除～之外
look to do   考慮做
look for   尋找
keep up with   趕上
get along well with   和～相處融洽
That's impressive!   真令人激賞!
a great deal of   很多的,大量的
a bit longer   (時間上)有點長
Will that be an issue for you?   這對你而言會是個問題嗎?
That won't be a problem at all.   那完全不是問題。
work late   工作到很晚
take care of   照顧

1 請聽《Track 12》並在括弧內填入正確答案。

  1. I've completed two technician certification courses (   )
    (   ) (   ) my bachelor's degree in Computer
    Science.

2. We (　　) (　　) (　　) the newest technology.

3. Do you (　　) (　　) (　　) with your co-workers?

4. There is a (　　) (　　) (　　) growth here.

5. Your company has a great reputation for (　　) (　　) (　　) its employees.

1 請再聽一次《Track 10》的會話後回答下面問題。

1. Jason 找新工作的理由之一為何?

　(A) 對目前的工作不滿

　(B) 想擔當更大的職責

　(C) 想擁有高收入

2. Jason 為什麼想在這家公司工作?

　(A) 因為它是快速成長且充滿活力的公司

　(B) 因為它是一流的企業

　(C) 因為它的工作環境很自由

3. Jason 對於工作時間抱持怎樣的想法?

　(A) 不想加班

　(B) 比一般工作時間長也沒關係

(C) 加班的部分希望能換取較長的有給薪休假

解答　　　　　　　　　　　　1.(B)　2.(A)　3.(B)

Speaking

會話

 請再聽一次《Track 10》。

Mr. Davis: Jason, will you tell me something about yourself?

Jason: Well, I've been interested in computers since I was a small child. We had PCs at home and Macs at school so I've used both my whole life. I've completed two technician certification courses in addition to my bachelor's degree in Computer Science.

Mr. Davis: Where do you currently work?

Jason: I'm a technician for Garrett Technologies.

Mr. Davis: Why are you looking to change jobs?

Jason: I'm looking for a position that gives me more responsibility and allows me to work with the very latest technology.

Mr. Davis: Yes, we keep up with the newest technology. Do you get along well with your co-workers?

Jason: Yes, of course. We work very closely together so we can complete projects efficiently. We have never missed a deadline.

Mr. Davis: That's impressive! Why do you want to work for our company specifically?

Jason: I've been reading a lot about this company in newspapers and business magazines recently and there is a great deal of growth here. I want to work for a company that is growing fast and exciting.

Mr. Davis: I see. The starting salary for this position is quite high, but our workdays are a bit longer than the typical workday. Will that be an issue for you?

Jason: No, Mr. Davis. That won't be a problem at all. I usually work late a few nights of the week anyway. Besides, your company has a great reputation for taking care of its employees.

中　譯 ···

戴維斯： 傑森，能否請你自我介紹一下？

傑　森： 嗯，我個人從小便對電腦充滿興趣。我家裡有個人電腦，學校有麥金塔的設備，因此我一直都有在用這兩種電腦。除了擁有資訊科學學士學位外，我也通過了另外兩個技術師檢定課程。

戴維斯： 你目前在哪裡工作？

傑　森： 我目前在葛瑞特科技公司擔任技術人員。

戴維斯： 是什麼原因促使你考慮換工作？

傑　森： 我一直在尋找一個能賦與我更大的責任，且可以與最新科技保持接觸的職位。

戴維斯：是的，我們公司一直走在科技的尖端。你和同事相處融洽嗎？

傑　森：相當融洽。我們在工作上合作無間而且很有效率，從來沒有延誤過任何工作。

戴維斯：這真令人激賞！你為什麼特別想來本公司工作呢？

傑　森：我最近透過多份報紙與商業雜誌得知，貴公司是一家非常具有成長力的公司，而我正想要在這樣一個成長迅速且又能激勵員工的地方工作。

戴維斯：我明白了。這個工作的起薪雖然很高，但每天工作的時間要比一般工作略久。這對你而言會構成問題嗎？

傑　森：不會，戴維斯先生，這一點完全不是問題。反正我經常一星期有幾個晚上要加班，更何況貴公司在業界向來以照顧員工著稱。

語　法

● 疑問句中也可以使用 something

疑問句中通常用 anything 而不用 something，但是當說話者肯定的語氣較強時，則使用 something，如會話中 Will you tell me *something* about yourself? 的句子。單純地詢問有沒有東西可以喝時，要用 Is there anything to drink?（有沒有什麼可以喝？）；若是心裡認為「應該有什麼可以喝才對」而發問時，則用 Is there *something* to drink?（有什麼可以喝？）。

● so that... 的 that 可以省略

so that 當作「（目的）為了」之意時，在口語中經常省略 that，例如會話中的句子：We work very closely together *so* we can complete projects efficiently.。再舉一例如下：Will you please speak up *so* (*that*) I can hear you better?（請你說話大聲點，這樣我可以聽得清楚些）。

Speaking Function 2

請對方提供訊息的說法

請聽《Track 13》。

1. A: Will you tell me something about your family?

   B: Well, it's a large one. There are seven of us children.

2. A: Do you know anything about helicopter tours?

   B: Well, this booklet will tell you all about them.

3. A: Which of these two laptops is better, do you think?

   B: I'm afraid I don't know anything about computers.

解說

● 希望對方能告知或談論某件事時，通常會用 Will you tell me about ～? 或 Can you tell me about ～? 的表達方式。更有禮貌的說法則用 Could you tell me about ～? 或 I wonder if you could tell me about ～.。若詢問不特定的人時，可用 Could anyone tell me about ～? 或 I wonder if someone could tell me about ～.。而在面試中經常使用 Will you tell me something about ～?（請你談談有關～）。

● Do you know about ～? 也是一種希望從對方那裡獲得訊息的表達方式，為「你知道有關～的事情嗎?」之意;「你知道任何有關～的事情嗎?」則是 Do you know anything about ～?。「或許你知道有關～的事情」即不預期對方會知道的情況下，說成 Do you happen to know about ～?, 或 Do you happen to know anything about ～?。語帶抱歉地說「不好意思打擾你，請問你知道有關～的事情?」是 Sorry to bother you, but do you know about ～?。此外，Have you got any idea about ～? 和 Do you know anything about ～? 的語意相同。

● 若要表示「我不知道，我不清楚」，其基本說法為 I don't know about

～.。想要使語氣更為和緩時，可以用 I'm afraid，說成 I'm afraid I don't know about ～.。若要強調對所詢問之事一無所知時，可用 I really don't know about ～ / I have no idea about ～ / I haven't got a clue about ～ / I haven't got the faintest idea about ～. 等句子。

練習 1【代換】

 請隨《Track 14》做代換練習。

1. *Will you tell me about*   the subway system in New York?

> Can you tell me about
> Could you tell me about
> Could anyone tell me about
> I wonder if you could tell me about
> I wonder if someone could tell me about

2. *Do you know about*   customs regulations in Japan?

> Do you know anything about
> Do you happen to know anything about
> Sorry to bother you, but do you know about
> Have you got any idea about

3. *I'm afraid I don't know anything about* Alaska Cruises.

> I don't know much about
> I really don't know about
> I have no idea about
> I haven't got a clue about
> I haven't got the faintest idea about

練習 2【角色扮演】

 請隨《Track 15》在嗶一聲後唸出灰色部分的句子。

1. A: Will you tell me something about your former company?
   B: Well, it's a computer software company specializing in computer graphics.

2. A: Do you know anything about Harbor Boat Tours?
   B: Well, this booklet will tell you all about them.

3. A: Which of these two golf courses is better, do you think?
   B: I'm afraid I don't know anything about golfing.

練習 3【覆誦重要語句】

 請隨《Track 16》覆誦英文句子。

1. my whole life 「我這一生」
   ↳ I've lived in New Orleans my whole life.
   （我這輩子一直都住在紐奧良。）

2. in addition to 「此外；除～之外」
   ↳ In addition to his film work, Mr. Adam does an occasional commercial.
   （除了電影工作之外，亞當先生偶爾也接拍廣告。）

3. currently 「目前，現在」
   ↳ He's currently editor in chief of *Newsweek*.
   （他是新聞週刊現任的總編輯。）

4. look to do 「考慮做」
   ↳ I'm looking to take a trip to Europe this summer.
   （我正在考慮今年夏天去歐洲度假。）

5. look for 「尋找」
   ↳ We're looking for a technician with a master's degree.
   （本公司正在徵求具有碩士學位的技術人員。）

6. get along well with 「與～相處融洽」
   ↳ Do you get along well with your mother-in-law?
   （你和你的岳母處得好嗎？）

7. so (that) 「為了」
   ↳ Open the window so you can get some fresh air.
   （請打開窗戶，呼吸一點新鮮空氣。）

8. deadline 「截止日期，最後期限」
   ↳ The deadline for deposits is June 21.
   （保證金的最後期限是六月二十一日。）

9. a great deal of 「很多的，大量的」
   ↳ It's a great deal of money.（這真是一大筆錢。）

10. bit 「稍許，一些」
   ↳ I think you're a bit too optimistic.
   （我認為你有點過於樂觀了。）

實力測驗

你是一家貿易公司的高級主管。公司將聘請一位熟悉中英貿易文化的外國人，而你是擔任面試的主考官。有位長期旅居台灣的外國人前來應徵，你想請他談談他所了解的台灣商業習慣，你該怎麼說呢？請練習以三種不同的說法詢問。

參考解答

1. Will you tell me something about business customs in Taiwan?
2. Could you tell me about business customs in Taiwan?
3. I wonder if you could tell me about business customs in Taiwan.

| Chapter 3 | Shopping Through the Internet | 網路購物 |

Listening

Warm-up / Pre-questions

 請聽《Track 17》的新聞快報後回答下面問題。

從新聞快報中我們得知什麼事？

(A) 網路購物增加了

(B) 有網路銀行開張了

(C) 和去年相比，消費者的購買力降低了

內容   A recent study conducted by the Consumers Advocacy Group reported that Internet shopping has increased 60% from last year.

中譯   由消費者保護團體最近所做的一項調查指出，網路購物已經較去年成長了百分之六十。

解答   (A)

解說   電視或報紙上的新聞報導常有時態不一致的情形，這是由於新聞大多是今天報導昨天發生的事，所以「現在發生的事」用現在式，「未來將發生的事」即用未來式。依此原則，即使主要子句的動詞 reported 採用了過去式，從屬子句的動詞依然可以如 has increased 採用現在完成式。

Listening Step 1

 請聽《Track 18》的會話後回答下面問題。

對話中的其中一人透過網路做什麼?

(A) 預約機位

(B) 開設網路書店

(C) 訂購父親的生日禮物

解答　　　　　　　　　　　　　　　　　　　　　　　(C)

Listening Step 2

熟悉下列關鍵字

shop	購物, 購買
business trip	出差
the internet	網際網路
order	訂購
ship	運送
item	商品
warehouse	倉庫
destination	目的地; 投送地點
besides	此外
convince	說服, 使相信
serious	認真的; 嚴重的
bookworm	書蟲, 非常愛好讀書的人
online bookstore	網路書店
gift certificate	禮券
access	接近; 進入或使用之權

① 請聽《Track 19》並在括弧內填入正確答案。

1. I'm leaving on Wednesday for a 2-week business (　　) to New York.
2. They have the items shipped out of a (　　) close to the order destination.
3. He is a serious (　　).
4. Just order him a gift (　　) and he can get whatever he wants.
5. He has Internet (　　), doesn't he?

解答

1. I'm leaving on Wednesday for a 2-week business (trip) to New York.
2. They have the items shipped out of a (warehouse) close to the order destination.
3. He is a serious (bookworm).
4. Just order him a gift (certificate) and he can get whatever he wants.
5. He has Internet (access), doesn't he?

① 請再聽一次《Track 18》的會話後回答下面問題。

1. 出差的地點是哪裡?
   (A) 紐約
   (B) 俄亥俄州
   (C) 國外
2. 生日禮物是什麼?
   (A) 國內旅遊券
   (B) 禮券
   (C) 書

Listening Step 3

熟悉下列語句

I forgot that...　我忘了…
What is the problem?　那有什麼關係? 有什麼問題嗎?
That is plenty of time to shop.　還有很充裕的時間可以購物。
go shopping　購物; 逛街
have it shipped to his house　使東西送到他家
in time　及時, 剛好
for a few extra dollars　多付一些錢
I'm convinced.　你說服了我。
whatever he wants　任何他想要的東西
get online　上線, 上網
right now　現在, 馬上

1 請聽《Track 20》並在括弧內填入正確答案。

1. I (　　) (　　　) my Dad's birthday is next week!

2. I won't have time to (　　) (　　).

3. Do you think that a gift would arrive in Ohio (　　)
(　　) if I ordered it today?

4. Besides, (　　) (　　) (　　) (　　　) dollars you can
have it shipped the next day.

5. I'm going to get online and order him a gift certificate
(　　) (　　).

解答
1. I (forgot) (that) my Dad's birthday is next week!
2. I won't have time to (go) (shopping).
3. Do you think that a gift would arrive in Ohio (in) (time) if I ordered it today?
4. Besides, (for) (a) (few) (extra) dollars you can have it shipped the next day.
5. I'm going to get online and order him a gift certificate (right) (now).

①)) 請再聽一次《Track 18》的會話後回答下面問題。

1. 對話中的人為什麼沒辦法自行採購禮物?
   (A) 因為汽車故障了
   (B) 因為要工作到很晚
   (C) 因為已經逼近出差時間了

2. 網路購物為什麼可以將商品很快送達?
   (A) 因為利用宅配服務
   (B) 因為從靠近送貨地點的倉庫出貨
   (C) 因為利用空運快遞

3. 為什麼最後決定送禮券?
   (A) 因為父親可以買自己喜歡的書
   (B) 因為比較便宜
   (C) 因為每年都送禮券

解答   1. (C)   2. (B)   3. (A)

Speaking

會話

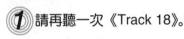 請再聽一次《Track 18》。

A: Oh, no! I forgot that my Dad's birthday is next week.

B: What is the problem? That is plenty of time to shop.

A: What is the problem? Don't you remember I'm leaving on Wednesday for a 2-week business trip to New York? I won't have time to go shopping.

B: Well, why don't you just order him something on the Internet and have it shipped to his house?

A: Do you think that a gift would arrive in Ohio in time if I ordered it today?

B: Of course! Ordering through the Internet is really fast. They have the items shipped out of a warehouse close to the order destination. Besides, for a few extra dollars you can have it shipped the next day.

A: All right. I'm convinced. Now, what do I get my Father?

B: What does he like to do?

A: He is a serious bookworm. He reads all the time.

B: That is so easy. Just order him a book from an online bookstore.

A: I'm not sure what he is reading these days though.

B: That is even easier. Just order him a gift certificate and he can get whatever he wants. He has Internet access, doesn't he?

A: Yes, he does. That is a great idea. I'm going to get online and order him a gift certificate right now.

A：糟了！我竟然忘記下星期就是我爸的生日了。

B：那有什麼關係？妳還有很多時間去買禮物。

A：有什麼關係？妳該不會不記得我星期三就要出差到紐約去兩個星期吧？我根本沒有時間去買禮物。

B：嗯，那麼妳何不上網訂購，再請網路公司直接將禮物送到妳父親那兒呢？

A：妳認為我今天訂貨，禮物就會來得及送達俄亥俄州嗎？

B：當然可以啦！在網路上訂購商品可是非常快速的。網路上的公司會從距離送貨目的地較近的倉庫出貨。除此之外，如果妳肯多花一點點錢，就算想要貨品明天就送到也沒問題。

A：好吧，妳說服我了。那麼，我該送我爸什麼禮物呢？

B：他平時的嗜好是什麼？

A：他是個不折不扣的書蟲，無時無刻都在閱讀。

B：那簡單，妳只需要到網路書店替他訂本書就可以了。

A：可是我實在不確定他最近讀的是哪一類的書。

B：那更好辦，妳可以直接訂購禮券給他，讓他選擇自己所喜歡的。他有在上網吧？

A：是的，他有。這真是一個好主意。我現在馬上就上網訂購禮券。

語　法

● I'm leaving on Wednesday... （我將於星期三出發…）
表示往來、出發、抵達等動詞的進行式，若與表示未來的副詞（片語）連用時，通常是表示不久的將來。如下例及會話中的句子：

We are going to the beach next Saturday.（我們將在下星期六去海灘。）

I'm leaving on Wednesday for a 2-week business trip to New York.

● 假設法過去式

假設法過去式通常像 If it were not rainy today, I would play tennis.（如果今天沒下雨，我會去打網球）這樣，用於與現在事實相反的情況；但有時也可用以表示現在或未來單純的假設，會話中的 Do you think that a gift would arrive in Ohio in time if I ordered it today? 即為一例。

● have + 受詞 + 過去分詞

They *have the items shipped* out of a warehouse close to the order destination. 中的 have 為使役動詞，為「使～被…」之意。另舉一例如下：I *had my hair cut.*（我剪了頭髮）。

Speaking Function 3

建議對方做～與不要做～的說法

 請聽《Track 21》。

1. A: I don't have time to go shopping.

   B: Why don't you do your shopping on the internet?

2. A: I'll come to see you at your office tomorrow afternoon.

   B: Fine, but just call me before you come.

3. A: Jim asked me if I could help him compile the statistics.

   B: I don't think you should help him.

解說

● 建議對方可以做什麼時，通常用 Why don't you ～？的說法。這是從「這樣做如何?」衍生成「你何不這樣做?」的敘述方式。熟人之間經常使用。

● 要對他人的行為提出建言，除了上述的表達方式之外，還可以用 Just ～或 I think you should ～等。Just ～是較為通俗的說法，和 Why don't you ～ ? 一樣用在較熟的人之間。若需要更有禮貌的表達時，可以用 If I were you, I'd ～ / It might be an idea to ～ / You would be wise to ～等說法。

● 建議對方最好不要做什麼，則使用否定句的形式，例如 I don't think you should ～ / Don't just ～ / I don't think you ought to ～等。若要更為有禮地建議，可用 If I were you, I wouldn't ～ / It's up to you, but I wouldn't ～等說法。

練習 1【代換】

 請隨《Track 22》做代換練習。

1. Why don't you *talk to your boss yourself?*

　　　　　　　　phone your supplier and complain?
　　　　　　　　try a Chinese restaurant?
　　　　　　　　ask Mary if she could help you?

2. *Just* 　　　　　call and see if the museum is open today.

I think you should
If I were you, I'd
It might be an idea to
You would be wise to

3. *I don't think you should* 　　　sell the stock now.

If I were you, I wouldn't
It's up to you, but I wouldn't
Don't just
I don't think you ought to

練習 2【角色扮演】

①請隨《Track 23》在嗶一聲後唸出灰色部分的句子。

1. A: My computer is old and giving me a lot of trouble.
   B: Why don't you buy a new one?
2. A: I'm not happy with my room.
   B: Just call the front desk and ask them to change your room.
3. A: I'm going to talk to my boss now.
   B: I don't think you should bother him now.

練習 3【覆誦重要語句】

①請隨《Track 24》覆誦英文句子。

1. plenty of 「很多」
   ↳ I've got plenty of time.（我有充裕的時間。）
2. go shopping 「購物」
   ↳ Let's go shopping this afternoon.
     （今天下午我們去購物吧。）
3. have + 受詞 + 過去分詞 「使（物）被…」
   ↳ I'd like to have it delivered to my house.
     （我要送貨到府的服務。）
4. in time 「及時，剛好」
   ↳ You're just in time.（你來得正好。）
5. for a few extra dollars 「多付少許金額」
   ↳ You can have a much better room for a few extra dollars.
     （只要多付一點點錢，房間就會好很多。）
6. convinced 「被說服，相信」

↳ I'm not convinced yet. （我還不能完全相信。）

7. whatever 「無論什麼」
   ↳ You can do whatever you want.
   （你可以做任何你想要做的事。）

8. access 「接近；進入或使用之權」
   ↳ The public doesn't have access to the room.
   （一般民眾不能進入這間房間。）

9. get online 「上線，上網」
   ↳ I'm going to get online and check the weather.
   （我要上網查詢天氣。）

10. right now 「現在，馬上」
    ↳ I'd like to see it right now. （我現在就要看。）

實力測驗

有位同事正負責一項企劃案，由於工作過多，擔心自己一個人無法在
期限之內順利完成，因而滿面愁容、憂心忡忡。請你以三種不同的說
法建議他和上司談談。

參考解答
1. Why don't you talk to your boss about the problem?
2. Just tell your boss about the problem.
3. If I were you, I would talk to the boss about your problem.

Chapter 4

Shipment Delay 出貨延遲

Listening

Warm-up / Pre-questions

 請聽《Track 25》的新聞快報後回答下面問題。

O'hare 國際機場發生什麼狀況？

(A) 因為下雪而被迫關閉

(B) 關閉了部分跑道

(C) 正開始進行除雪作業，但不知何時才會重新開放

內容 Chicago's O'hare International Airport was closed due to severe winter storms dumping heavy snow on runways.

中譯 因為嚴重的冬季暴風雪來襲，跑道積雪，造成芝加哥歐海爾國際機場關閉。

解答 (A)

解說 無生物的專有名詞或普通名詞可以直接加上 's 構成所有格。特別是報紙或是廣播、電視上的新聞報導，經常使用如 Chicago's O'hare International Airport 中出現的無生物所有格。due to 為「因為」、severe 為「嚴重的」、dump 為「傾盆而下」、runway 則為「跑道」之意。

Listening Step 1

 請聽《Track 26》的會話後回答下面問題。

Bill 正在做什麼？
  (A) 加訂零件
  (B) 詢問零件為何遲遲不來
  (C) 因零件出貨太慢，正要取消訂購

解答   (B)

Listening Step 2

熟悉下列關鍵字

actually   實際上，事實上
complain   抱怨，投訴
delivery service   送貨服務
order   訂購，訂貨
standard plastic stereo feet   標準規格的音響塑膠基座
shipment   裝載的貨物
nasty   惡劣的，很壞的
impact   影響，衝擊
delivery schedule   交貨時程
delay   延誤，延遲
part   零件
manufacture   製造，生產
product   產品
frustration   挫折，沮喪
ground delivery   陸上運送
customer   顧客，客戶
e-mail   電子郵件
explain   解釋，說明
apologize   致歉

weather conditions 　天氣狀況
patience 　耐心，忍耐

1 請聽《Track 27》並在括弧內填入正確答案。

1. I'm actually calling to (　　　) about your delivery service.

2. The nasty weather here has really (　　　) our delivery schedule.

3. I'm sure they have heard these weather (　　　) on the news.

4. Please call me as soon as my (　　　) is on the way.

5. Thanks for your (　　　).

解答

1. I'm actually calling to (complain) about your delivery service.

2. The nasty weather here has really (impacted) our delivery schedule.

3. I'm sure they have heard these weather (conditions) on the news.

4. Please call me as soon as my (shipment) is on the way.

5. Thanks for your (patience).

1 請再聽一次《Track 26》的會話後回答下面問題。

1. 什麼東西沒送來？

　(A) 電子郵件

　(B) 交貨計畫表

　(C) 音響的零件

2. Bill 對 Comet 塑膠公司做了怎樣的要求？

　(A) 希望能優先寄送零件

(B) 未能準時送達的商品希望能打個折扣

(C) 一旦零件可以寄送的話請與其聯絡

解答　　　　　　　　　　　　　　　1. (C)　2. (C)

Listening Step 3

熟悉下列語句

How may I help you?　有什麼是我能為您服務的嗎？
What can I do for you?　我能為你做什麼嗎？
I'm calling to...　我打電話來是要…
there's not much we can do　我們實在幫不上什麼忙
This just won't do.　這樣不行。
count on　倚靠，依賴
out of control　失去掌控，不能控制
as well　也
deal with　處理
apologize for　為～致歉
on the news　在新聞中
as soon as　立刻；只要～便馬上
on the way　在途中
get ～ to...　使～送達…

1 請聽《Track 28》並在括弧內填入正確答案。

1. There's (　　) (　　　　) we can do until the weather clears up.

2. This just (　　　) (　　　).

3. I really (　　　) (　　　) the plastic parts from your

company to manufacture my products.

4. It's really ( ) ( ) ( ) ( ).

5. Please call me as soon as my shipment is ( ) ( )
( ).

1 請再聽一次《Track 26》的會話後回答下面問題。

1. 為什麼零件無法準時出貨?

(A) 因為天候惡劣

(B) 因為交通阻塞

(C) 因為罷工導致機場關閉

2. Comet 塑膠公司對於顧客做了怎樣的緊急應變處理?

(A) 還沒採取任何應變措施

(B) 發出電子郵件通知顧客會儘快送達

(C) 發出電子郵件說明無法準時送達的理由並向顧客道歉

3. Bill 決定之後要怎麼做呢?

(A) 向上司說明該批零件無法準時送達

(B) 等 Comet 塑膠公司的電話通知

(C) 考慮購買別家公司的零件

解答   1. (A)   2. (C)   3. (B)

Speaking

會話

 請再聽一次《Track 26》。

Secretary: Good afternoon. Comet Plastics Inc. This is Shelly Speaking. How may I help you?

Bill: Hi, Shelly. This is Bill Scott from Paramount Sound Systems.

Secretary: Hello, Bill, and what can I do for you?

Bill: I'm actually calling to complain about your delivery service. I ordered 40 thousand of your standard plastic stereo feet last week, but I still haven't received the shipment yet.

Secretary: I'm sorry, Bill, but the nasty weather here has really impacted our delivery schedule.

Bill: What can you do about this delay? I have a warehouse full of stereos with no plastic feet on them. I can't sell them like this!

Secretary: I'm sorry, but there's not much we can do until the weather clears up.

Bill: This just won't do. I really count on the plastic parts from your company to manufacture my products.

Secretary: I understand your frustration, Bill, but ground delivery has trickled to a stop and now the airport is closed. It's really out of our control. Many other customers have been impacted as well.

Bill: How are you dealing with all of these unhappy customers?

Secretary: We've just sent all of our customers e-mails explaining what has happened and apologizing for the delay. I'm sure they have heard these weather conditions on the news.

Bill: Well, I suppose I'll just have to wait, then. Please call me as soon as my shipment is on the way.

Secretary: Sure, I will. We'll get your order to you as soon as we can. Thanks for your patience, Bill.

中　譯 ···

秘書：午安！這裡是慧星塑膠股份有限公司，我是雪莉。有什麼需要為您服務的嗎？

比爾：嗨，雪莉。我是派拉蒙音響公司的比爾・史考特。

秘書：你好！比爾，有什麼是我能為你效勞的嗎？

比爾：事實上我是打電話來投訴你們的送貨服務的。我訂了四萬個貴公司的標準規格音響塑膠基座，但是到現在都還沒收到貨。

秘書：非常抱歉，比爾，不過這裡的惡劣天候確實影響我們的交貨時程。

比爾：有沒有辦法能夠解決這送貨延誤的問題啊？我有一整個倉庫裝滿了只缺塑膠基座的音響，這樣我沒辦法出貨啊！

秘書：真是抱歉！不過在天氣轉晴之前，我們實在幫不上什麼忙。

比爾：這樣怎麼行呢，我真的急需你們的塑膠零件來完成產品製造。

秘書：比爾，我能體會你懊惱不滿的心情，不過，這實在不是我們所能掌控的。陸上配送系統已經幾乎癱瘓，而現在就連機場也關閉了。還有許多其他的客戶也同樣受到影響。

比爾： 你們是如何應付所有不悅的客戶呢?

秘書： 我們已經透過電子郵件發函給所有的客戶，向他們解釋狀況並且為延誤的送貨服務致歉。我相信客戶們必定也從新聞中聽說了天氣的狀況。

比爾： 好吧，那麼我想除了等待，好像也沒有別的辦法了。只要貨一上路，就請立刻打電話跟我聯絡。

秘書： 沒問題。只要情況許可，我們會儘快將你訂的貨送達。比爾，非常感謝你的耐心等待。

語　法 ....

● 「有用」之意的 do
  動詞的 do 與助動詞 will 連用，表示「有用」、「合適」、「足夠」之意。例如「這樣行嗎?」說成 Will this *do*?，回答「這樣就行」則說 This will *do*.。若要說「這樣不行」是 This won't *do*.，再加以強調便是 This just won't *do*.。

Speaking Function 4

抱怨、表示不滿的說法

請聽《Track 29》。

1. A: Yes, Ma'am?

   B: I want to complain about this watch I bought yesterday.

2. A: I'm sorry. We can't replace it with a new one.

   B: Well, this is most unsatisfactory. I'd like to speak to the manager.

3. A: I'm fed up with the noises the airconditioner is making.

   B: I'll send our repairman to your room right away.

解說
- 抱怨時，若要說得直接了當，可用 I want to complain about ～，about 的後面直接接要抱怨的內容。例如新買的皮包有刮傷的痕跡時，可以直接向店員說 I want to complain about the bag I bought yesterday.；若是打電話去抱怨，可用 call 這個字，說成 I'm calling to complain about the bag I bought yesterday. 即可。complain 的名詞為 complaint，可以使用此名詞形將句子改為 I've got a complaint about ～或 I have a complaint to make about ～，兩句句意相同。
- 要向對方表示不滿或無法認同對方意見時，可以說 That is most unsatisfactory.。此外，That just isn't good enough. 或是 That won't do. 也是適合抱怨時說出的句子。That's the limit!（已經忍無可忍了）和 That really is the limit! 則是不滿達到極限時的抱怨語句。
- 另外，可以用「厭煩」的動詞片語 fed up with 來表達不滿的情緒。例如已經聽膩了朋友無聊的笑話時，可以用 I'm fed up with your poor puns. 來表示。相同的意思還可以用 have (just about) had enough of 造句表達，如 I've (just about) had enough of your sarcasm.（我已經受夠了你的譏諷）。若要催促他人去做某事時，則使用 Something must be done about ～ 或 You've got to do something about ～的表達方式。

練習 1【代換】

①請隨《Track 30》做代換練習。

1. *I'm calling to complain*   about your delivery service.
   I want to complain
   I've got a complaint
   I have a complaint to make

2. That *is most unsatisfactory.*
       just isn't good enough.
       won't do.
       just won't do.
       really is the limit!

3. *I'm fed up with*   the noises upstairs.
   I've just about had enough of
   Something must be done about
   You've got to do something about

練習 2 【角色扮演】

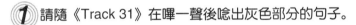 請隨《Track 31》在嗶一聲後唸出灰色部分的句子。

1. A: Yes, Ma'am?
   B: I want to complain about this hat I bought yesterday.
2. A: I'm sorry. We don't have your name on the waiting list.
   B: Well, this is most unsatisfactory. I'd like to speak to the
      person in charge.
3. A: I'm fed up with your bad service.
   B: I'm very sorry. We're trying to improve it now.

練習 3【覆誦重要語句】

1 請隨《Track 32》覆誦英文句子。

1. call to 「打電話來是為了」
   ↳ I'm calling to reconfirm my reservation.
   （我打電話來是為了要再確認一下我的預約。）

2. impact 「影響，衝擊」
   ↳ The crops were impacted by the bad weather.
   （農作物受到惡劣氣候的影響。）

3. there's not much one can do 「（人）沒什麼可以幫得上忙的」
   ↳ There's not much I can do about it.
   （實在沒什麼是我可以幫得上忙的。）

4. do 「有用」
   ↳ Will this do?（這麼做有用嗎?）

5. count on 「倚靠，依賴」
   ↳ I count on your support.（我全靠你的支持了。）

6. out of control 「失去掌控，不能控制」
   ↳ The children are out of my control.
   （我管不住這些孩子了。）

7. deal with 「處理」
   ↳ I don't know how to deal with the situation.
   （我實在不知道該如何處理這種狀況。）

8. on the news 「在新聞中」
   ↳ I heard the accident on the news.
   （我在新聞報導中得知這則意外的消息。）

9. on the way 「在途中」
   ↳ The parts you ordered are on the way.

（你訂購的零件已經在路上了。）
10. get ～ to... 「使～送達⋯」
　　↳ I'll get the photos to you as soon as they are developed.
　　（照片只要一洗好，我就會立刻送去給你。）

實力測驗

你利用郵購買了毛衣，但是沒想到寄來的尺寸比當初訂購的尺寸小。
請試以三種不同的說法向郵購公司抱怨寄錯的情形。

參考解答
1. I'm calling to complain about the sweater I bought by mail order.
　 You sent me a smaller size than I ordered.
2. Hello. I want to complain about the sweater I bought by mail
　 order. You sent me a smaller size than I ordered.
3. Hello. I've got a complaint about the sweater I bought by mail
　 order. You sent me a smaller size than I ordered.

Brunch 早午餐

Listening

Warm-up / Pre-questions

 請聽《Track 33》的商業廣告後回答下面問題。

早午餐的時間是幾點到幾點?
(A) 早上 9 點到下午 1 點
(B) 早上 10 點到下午 2 點
(C) 早上 10 點到下午 3 點

內容　George's Broiler is now serving an elegant brunch on Sundays from 10 a.m. until 2 p.m. Come and join us for a fine dining experience.

中譯　喬治燒烤餐廳現正推出豪華早午餐,服務時間由每星期日早上 10 點到下午 2 點。快來喬治享受美好的用餐吧!

解答　(B)

解說　George's Broiler 是餐廳的名字。請留意利用所有格構成餐廳名字的用法。on Sunday 是「在星期天」的意思,若在 Sunday 後面加上 s 變成 on Sundays,則是指「在所有的星期天」,也就是「在每個星期天」的意思。brunch 是 breakfast 和 lunch 的複合字,指的是兼具早餐與午餐的一餐,餐廳通常在禮拜天的上午 10 點到下午 2 點會推出這樣的服務。broiler 為「烤肉用的器具」、serve 為「推出(餐飲服務等)」、elegant 為「非常棒的」、dining 為「用餐」、experience 則為「經驗」之意。

Listening Step 1

請聽《Track 34》的會話後回答下面問題。

> Ellen 想要做什麼？
>
> (A) 想要多睡一會兒
>
> (B) 想自己一個人去吃早午餐
>
> (C) 想和 Rachel 一起去吃早午餐
>
> 解答   (C)

Listening Step 2

熟悉下列關鍵字

wake	喚醒，弄醒
sleep-deprived	睡眠不足
last	持續
kid	開玩笑
champagne	香檳酒
appealing	有吸引力的，有誘惑力的
convincing	有說服力的，令人信服的
single	單身的
good-looking	樣貌姣好的，好看的（除女性外，亦可用來形容男性）
self-conscious	介意他人目光的，害羞的
forever	永遠
fun	愉悅，開心
promise	承諾，保證

① 請聽《Track 35》並在括弧內填入正確答案。

1. Did I (　　　) you up?
2. I know, but brunch (　　　) until 2.
3. I heard that a lot of (　　　) people go there on Sundays.
4. You might meet a (　　　　) guy there.
5. You'll have (　　).

解答

1. Did I (wake) you up?
2. I know, but brunch (lasts) until 2.
3. I heard that a lot of (single) people go there on Sundays.
4. You might meet a (good-looking) guy there.
5. You'll have (fun).

① 請再聽一次《Track 34》的會話後回答下面問題。

1. Rachel 現在在哪裡?
   (A) 還躺在床上
   (B) 在廚房
   (C) 在飯廳

2. Rachel 要花多久時間才能準備好?
   (A) 20 分鐘
   (B) 30 分鐘
   (C) 1 小時

解答　　　　　　　　　　　　　　　　　1. (A)　2. (C)

Listening Step 3

熟悉下列語句

catch up on 趕上，補足
sleep away 睡掉，藉睡眠打發時間
That doesn't sound like a bad idea. 這主意聽起來不錯。
try out 試試看
in bed 躺在床上
You must be kidding. 你一定是在開玩笑吧!
for starters 第一點，首先
just this once 僅此一次
in one hour 一小時後

1 請聽《Track 36》並在括弧內填入正確答案。

1. I was trying to (　　) (　　) (　　) some sleep from a busy week.
2. That doesn't (　　) (　　) a bad idea.
3. I wanted to (　　) (　　) the new brunch at George's Broiler today.
4. Well, (　　) (　　), I heard the food is great.
5. Come on Rachel. Please go (　　) (　　) (　　).

解答
1. I was trying to (catch) (up) (on) some sleep from a busy week.
2. That doesn't (sound) (like) a bad idea.
3. I wanted to (try) (out) the new brunch at George's Broiler today.
4. Well, (for) (starters), I heard the food is great.
5. Come on Rachel. Please go (just) (this) (once).

請再聽一次《Track 34》的會話後回答下面問題。

1. Rachel 為什麼睡眠不足?
   (A) 因為前一天參加派對到很晚才回來
   (B) 因為前一天工作到很晚才回來
   (C) 因為上禮拜的工作很忙
2. Ellen 為什麼要邀請 Rachel 去吃早午餐?
   (A) 因為不想自己一個人去
   (B) 因為是非常好的餐廳,無論如何都想帶 Rachel 去
   (C) 因為想藉由吃飯的機會介紹朋友給 Rachel 認識
3. Rachel 為什麼改變心意決定去吃早午餐?
   (A) 因為美味的料理和香檳酒實在深具吸引力
   (B) 因為或許會遇見帥哥也說不定
   (C) 因為可以和 Ellen 的朋友一起用餐

解答 　　　　　　　　　　　　　　1. (C)　　2. (A)　　3. (B)

Speaking

會話

請再聽一次《Track 34》。

Ellen: Hi, Rachel. Did I wake you up?

Rachel: Oh, hi, Ellen. Yes, you did wake me. I was trying to catch up on some sleep from a busy week.

Ellen: But it is 11 o'clock! Are you going to sleep your whole

Sunday away?

Rachel: That doesn't sound like a bad idea. I'm really sleep-deprived. What are you doing?

Ellen: Well, I wanted to try out the new brunch at George's Broiler today, but I don't want to go by myself. Won't you come with me, please?

Rachel: Ellen, I'm still in bed!

Ellen: I know, but brunch lasts until 2. That's plenty of time for you to get ready.

Rachel: You must be kidding, Ellen. Why would I want to go to brunch when I could be sleeping?

Ellen: Well, for starters, I heard the food is great. Besides, they have champagne.

Rachel: Good food and champagne, that is appealing but not convincing.

Ellen: Besides the good food and champagne, I heard that a lot of single people go there on Sundays. You might meet a good-looking guy there.

Rachel: Now I'll be really self-conscious. It'll take me forever to get ready!

Ellen: Come on Rachel. Please go just this once. You'll have fun. I promise.

Rachel: Oh, all right. I'll be ready in one hour.

中 譯

愛倫：嗨，瑞秋，我是不是把妳給吵醒啦？

瑞秋：嗨，愛倫，是啊，妳的確把我給吵醒了。上禮拜實在是太忙碌了，我現在在補眠。

愛倫：可是現在已經十一點了耶！妳不會要把整個星期天浪費在睡覺上吧？

瑞秋：這主意也不壞啊。我實在是睡眠不足。妳要做什麼？

愛倫：嗯，我想去試試喬治燒烤餐廳新推出的早午餐，不過我不太想一個人去，妳要不要一起來呀？拜託嘛！

瑞秋：愛倫，我現在還躺在床上呢。

愛倫：我知道，不過早午餐的服務到下午兩點才結束，妳還有充分的時間可以準備。

瑞秋：愛倫，妳不是在開玩笑吧！我睡得正舒服，有什麼理由要跟妳去吃早午餐？

愛倫：首先，我聽說那兒的食物很棒。再者，他們還提供香檳喔。

瑞秋：美食加香檳，是很誘人，不過說服力還不夠。

愛倫：除了美食和香檳，我還聽說每星期日都有很多單身漢會去那兒，說不定妳會遇見帥哥喔。

瑞秋：那我可會在意其他人的眼光了，我想我永遠沒法準備好的。

愛倫：別這樣嘛，瑞秋。去這一次就好，我保證妳會很開心的。

瑞秋：好吧好吧，我大概一個小時後就準備好。

語　法

● 使用助動詞 do (does, did) 的強調句

肯定句中有時將助動詞 do (does, did) 放在動詞原形前面，用以強調動詞。平常我們會說 Yes, you woke me.；若要強調動詞「被吵醒」，就變成 Yes, you *did* wake me.。其他例句如：I hope so.，若要強調「我真心地期盼」，就說 I *do* hope so.。又例如：He knows it.，想要強調動詞「知道」，就說 He *does* know it.。

- 修辭性疑問

  「為什麼我要做～呢?(不要,不想做)」,像這樣用反問的語氣將自
  己的意識或感情強烈地傳達給對方的構句方式稱作修辭性疑問。上
  面對話中 Why would I want to go to brunch when I could be sleeping?
  「我睡得正舒服,有什麼理由要跟你去吃早午餐?(我才不要,沒有
  道理這麼做嘛。)」正是修辭性疑問的構句。

Speaking Function 5

勸誘、說服的說法

請聽《Track 37》。

1. A: I don't want to go there by myself. Won't you come with
      me, please?
   B: I wish I could, but I've already got an appointment.
2. A: Please attend the meeting just this once.
   B: Well, all right, if you insist.
3. A: Can I persuade you to sacrifice your golf date?
   B: Absolutely not. It's a very important golf date.

解說
- 希望促使對方做某事時,只要在 Won't you ～ ? 之後加上 please
  就成了強烈的勸誘句。這種句型經常用於勸說對方。希望對方一
  起前往的勸誘句可以說成 Won't you come with me, please?;希望
  對方讓自己加入是 Won't you let me in, please?,希望能坐上巴士
  則是 Won't you let me on, please?。
- 添加 just this once 或 just for me 等用語時,表示更強力地促使對
  方做某事,其用法如 Will you please lend me some money just this

once?（可不可以請你借我一點錢，就這一次就好）。添加「拜託」之意的 for my sake / for Pete's sake / for goodness' sake / for Heaven's sake / for God's sake 等語句也可以用來加強語意。

● 要表示「勸說、說服」之意時，可以直接用 persuade 這個字促使對方做出行動。其相關語句如下：Can I persuade you ～? / Can't I persuade you ～? / Could I persuade you ～? / Couldn't I persuade you ～? / Could you be persuaded ～?。其中 can 與 could 的差別，在於用 could 比用 can 更有禮貌。

練習 1【代換】

 請隨《Track 38》做代換練習。

1. Won't you *come with me, please?*

> sit down, please?
> come to dinner, please?
> join us for a drink, please?
> let me in, please?

2. Please attend the meeting *just this once!*

> just for me!
> for my sake!
> for Pete's sake!
> for goodness' sake!
> for Heaven's sake!
> for God's sake!

3. *Can I persuade you* to sacrifice your golf date?

> Can't I persuade you
> Could I persuade you

Couldn't I persuade you
Could you be persuaded

練習 2【角色扮演】

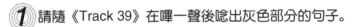 請隨《Track 39》在嗶一聲後唸出灰色部分的句子。

1. A: I don't want to go there alone. Won't you come with me, please?

   B: I wish I could, but I've already got an appointment.

2. A: Please lend me your camera just this once.

   B: Well, all right, if you promise not to break it.

3. A: Can I persuade you to cancel the trip?

   B: I don't think so. I've been looking forward to it for a long time.

練習 3【覆誦重要語句】

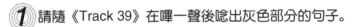 請隨《Track 40》覆誦英文句子。

1. wake ～ (up) 「叫醒」
   ↳ Will you wake me up at 6 tomorrow morning?
   （可以請你明天早上六點鐘叫我起床嗎?）

2. catch up on 「趕上，補足」
   ↳ I have some work to catch up on.
   （我還有一些工作要趕。）

3. sound like 「聽起來，似乎」
   ↳ It sounds like a very good idea.
   （這聽起來真是個好主意。）

4. try out 「試試看」
   ↳ I'd like to try out the new Chinese restaurant on West Street.（我想去西街新開的那家中國餐廳吃看看。）

5. in bed 「躺在床上」
   ↳ I'm sick in bed.（我臥病在床。）

6. last 「持續；直到」
   ↳ The musical lasts 2 hours.（這齣音樂劇長達兩小時。）

7. kid 「開玩笑」
   ↳ No kidding.（別開玩笑。）

8. for starters 「第一點，首先」
   ↳ For starters, the food is very cheap.
   （首先，這食物非常便宜。）

9. have fun 「愉悅，開心」
   ↳ I had a lot of fun riding a variety of rides in the amusement park.
   （我在遊樂園乘坐了多項遊樂設施，玩得很開心。）

10. in one hour 「一小時後」
    ↳ This will be finished in one hour.
    （這會在一小時後結束。）

實力測驗

同事為工作上的事和上司大吵了一架，並揚言要遞出辭呈，請以三種不同的說法勸他別這樣。

參考解答
1. Won't you reconsider handing in your resignation, please?
2. Come on! Please reconsider handing in your resignation for God's sake.
3. Can't I persuade you to reconsider handing in your resignation?

Chapter 6	**Inventory**	庫　存

Listening

Warm-up / Pre-questions

 請聽完《Track 41》的新聞快報後回答下面問題。

這個城鎮週末將舉行什麼活動?
- (A) 舊書拍賣會
- (B) 國際書展
- (C) 書商協會的年度大會

內容　This weekend's 57th annual convention of the American Booksellers Association is expected to bring about 7,000 travelers to the downtown area.

中譯　本週末在市中心舉行的第五十七屆全美書商協會年度大會,預期將帶來約七千名的遊客。

解答　(C)

解說　be expected to do 為「預期將會~」之意的片語。downtown 是指「商業或經濟的中心地」,而 annual 為「週年的,一年一度的」、convention 為「大會」、bookseller 為「書商,書籍販售業者」、association 則為「協會」之意。

Listening Step 1

 請聽《Track 42》的會話後回答下面問題。

Mr. Douglas 正在檢查什麼?
  (A) 影印紙的庫存
  (B) 影印機
  (C) 大會的場地

解答 (A)

Listening Step 2

熟悉下列關鍵字

supply room 儲藏室
inventory 庫存
concerned 擔心的, 關心的
copy paper 影印紙
remember 記得
additional 追加的; 額外的
discuss 討論, 談及
participant 參加者, 與會者
service 服務
invoice 發貨單, 發票
supply 提供, 供給
needs 需要, 需求
status 狀態, 狀況

①請聽《Track 43》並在括弧內填入正確答案。

1. I'm in the supply room looking over the (   ).
2. I remember quite clearly that I ordered an (   ) 8 boxes last week.

3. We were discussing how many convention (　　　　) would be using our services.

4. Let me pull out the (　　　) now.

5. I'll call you back with the (　　　) of the order.

1 請再聽一次《Track 42》的會話後回答下面問題。

1. Jennifer 追加訂購了幾箱影印紙?

　(A) 6 箱

　(B) 8 箱

　(C) 12 箱

2. Mr. Douglas 請 Jennifer 做什麼事?

　(A) 請她再訂 8 箱的影印紙

　(B) 請她打電話轉告對方希望影印紙能在今天下午送達

　(C) 請她打電話問一下加訂的影印紙送出了沒

Listening Step 3

熟悉下列語句

look over 仔細檢查（物品等）；瀏覽（文件等）
because of 因為，由於
What seems to be the problem? 有什麼問題嗎？
pull out 取出
need you to... 需要你…
make sure 確定，確認
hold a convention 舉行大會
call back 回電話
the status of the order 訂購的情形

1 請聽《Track 44》並在括弧內填入正確答案。

1. I'm in the supply room (   ) (   ) the inventory.
2. What (   ) (   ) (   ) the problem?
3. I (   ) (   ) (   ) call them right now.
4. (   ) (   ) the shipment gets delivered this afternoon.
5. I'll (   ) (   ) (   ) with the status of the order.

解答

1. I'm in the supply room (looking)(over) the inventory.
2. What (seems) (to) (be) the problem?
3. I (need) (you) (to) call them right now.
4. (Make) (sure) the shipment gets delivered this afternoon.
5. I'll (call) (you) (back) with the status of the order.

1 請再聽一次《Track 42》的會話後回答下面問題。

1. 為什麼影印紙一定得準備充足？
   (A) 因為要擴大商業規模

(B) 因為書商協會的大會將在旅館召開

(C) 因為要在書商協會的大會上分發大量的影印廣告傳單

2. 如何得知影印紙沒有送到的這件事？

(A) 查看了發貨單

(B) 曾打電話到訂購的公司詢問

(C) 找遍儲藏室的每個角落

3. Jennifer 在催促影印紙公司送貨之後，會做什麼動作？

(A) 打電話給老闆

(B) 整理儲藏室

(C) 和要在旅館舉辦大會的負責人取得聯絡

解答　　　　　　　　　　　　　　1. (B)　2. (A)　3. (A)

Speaking

會話

 請再聽一次《Track 42》。

Receptionist: Hello and welcome to the Parkway Hotel's business center. This is Jennifer. May I help you?

Boss: Hi, Jennifer. This is Mr. Douglas. I'm in the supply room looking over the inventory because of the convention coming to town this weekend and I'm really concerned.

Receptionist: Why? What seems to be the problem?

Boss: Well, We only have 12 boxes of copy paper and I don't think that's enough for the weekend.

Receptionist: I remember quite clearly that I ordered an additional 8 boxes last week when we were discussing how many convention participants would be using our services.

Boss: Where are the boxes then?

Receptionist: I don't know. Let me pull out the invoice now.

Boss: All right. I'll wait.

(*A few seconds later*)

Receptionist: The invoice is right here, Mr. Douglas. I did order those boxes of copy paper. They just haven't been delivered yet.

Boss: Jennifer, I need you to call them right now and make sure the shipment gets delivered this afternoon. This will be the last time the American Booksellers Association holds a convention in our hotel if we can't even supply their copy needs.

Receptionist: Yes, Sir. I'll call them right now and then call you back with the status of the order.

Boss: Thank you.

中　譯 ....

接待員：您好，這裡是帕克威飯店商務中心，我是珍妮佛，能為您效勞嗎？

老　闆：嗨，珍妮佛，我是道格拉斯先生。我現在正在儲藏室檢查庫存，大會在這個週末就要舉行了，我實在非常擔心。

接待員：為什麼？有什麼問題嗎？

老　闆：我們目前只剩下十二箱的影印紙，我不認為這足以應付這個週末的需求。

接待員：我非常確定當我們上週談到與會者的服務需求量時，我有再加訂八箱的影印紙。

老　闆：那麼現在這些紙在哪裡？

接待員：我不清楚，讓我把發貨單調出來看看。

老　闆：沒關係，我等妳。

（一會兒過後）

接待員：道格拉斯先生，發貨單在這。我的確訂了八箱的影印紙，不過貨還沒有送到。

老　闆：珍妮佛，我要妳立刻打電話跟對方確認貨會在今天下午送到。假如我們連全美書商協會影印方面的需求都滿足不了的話，今年恐怕將會是他們最後一次選擇在本飯店舉行大會了。

接待員：是的，老闆。我現在立刻撥電話過去，之後我會再撥電話給您回報訂購的情形。

老　闆：謝謝。

語　法

● 電話中自己的名字之前要加 Mr. 或 Mrs.

如同 This is Mr. Smith. 或 This is Mrs. Smith. 般，在電話中即使是報上自己的姓名也要加上 Mr. 或 Mrs.。在美國，雖然工作場合中一般都習慣直呼其名，但是當上司打電話給部屬時，還是會在自己的名字之前加上 Mr. 或 Mrs.。

● get + 過去分詞

get + 過去分詞為「被～」之意，例如皮包被偷了，可以說 My bag *got stolen.*，而會話中的 make sure the shipment *gets delivered* 則為「確定貨物被送達」之意。

Speaking Function 6

 請聽《Track 45》。

1. A: What color was the jacket he was wearing?

   B: Let me think. Yes, I remember. It was brown. Light brown.

2. A: Do you remember the make of the car?

   B: Yes, it was a Ford.

3. A: How was the subcommittee meeting?

   B: Oh, no! I forgot that there was a meeting this morning.

解說

● 要表達努力地記住不忘或是想起了什麼事情,都可以用 remember 這個字。例如想起鑰匙放在哪裡,可以說 Now I remember where I put the keys.。對於某件事情記得非常清楚時,可以說 I remember it very well.;另外也可以用 I remember that... 的句型來造句,例如: I remember that he used to go fishing on Sunday. (我記得他以前經常在星期天去釣魚)。若要表示「記得過去曾經~」時,要用 remember 加現在分詞的形式,例如: I remember seeing him somewhere. (我記得好像在哪裡見過他)。此外,還可以用 remember + 人 + 現在分詞的形式來表示「記得某人曾經~」,例如: I remember her saying so. (我記得她是這樣說的)。當然,也可以用 well 或 quite clearly 等副詞來強調記得非常清楚。As far as I remember (就我記憶所及) / What I remember is that... (我記得的是…) / If I remember correctly (如果我沒記錯的話) 等也都是一些經常慣用的說法。

● 當要詢問對方是否記得某件事時,最普遍的說法便是 Do you remember...?,客氣一點的說法則為 I wonder if you remember...?。

親近的朋友之間還可以用 Don't you remember...? 或 Have you forgotten...? 等略為直率的反問講法。如果想表示「有沒有可能突然想起已經忘記的事情」，可以利用 by any chance 的說法，例如詢問他人：Do you by any chance remember...?。而下面這一句 Do you remember the make of the car? 中的 make 是指「～製」、「廠牌」，句意是「你記得那輛汽車是哪一家公司生產的嗎?」。此外，a Ford 已經變成專有名詞，一定要加不定冠詞 a，表示「福特汽車」之意。

● 忘了某件事情但是現在才想起來的時候，要用過去式 I forgot。例如「忘了早上要開會」要說成 I forgot there was a meeting this morning.。若要表示忘了該去做某件事時，則要像 I forgot to call him this afternoon.（我忘了今天下午要打電話給他）的用法，在 forgot 的後面接續 to 不定詞。

● 如果是忘記了而且再也想不起來的時候，則要用現在式 I forget，例如：I forget his name.（我忘了他的名字）。如果用現在完成式 I've forgotten his name. 則是更加強調「完全忘記了、一點兒也想不起來」的語氣。I can't remember... 或是 I don't remember... 也是想不起來的時候經常使用的說法。

練習 1【代換】

 請隨《Track 46》做代換練習。

1. *I remember*　　　　　　　　that I ordered five boxes of copy paper on Monday.

> I remember quite clearly
> I distinctly remember
> I vaguely remember
> What I remember is

2. *Do you remember*   the name of the restaurant?

Do you by any chance remember

Don't you remember

Have you forgotten

I wonder if you remember

3. I forgot *that there was a meeting this morning.*

that I was supposed to lock the front door.

that he is coming today.

to mail the letter.

all about it.

4. *I forget*   where I met him.

I've forgotten

I've completely forgotten

I don't remember

I can't remember

練習 2【角色扮演】

請隨《Track 47》在嗶一聲後唸出灰色部分的句子。

1. A: What color was the car he was driving?

   B: Let me think. Yes, I remember. It was green. Dark green.

2. A: Do you remember what he said?

   B: Yes, he said he would donate 10,000 dollars.

3. A: How was the directors' meeting?

   B: Oh, no! I forgot that there was a meeting this morning.

練習 3【覆誦重要語句】

1 請隨《Track 48》覆誦英文句子。

1. look over 「仔細檢查」
   ↳ She is busy looking over invoices.
   （她正忙著檢查發貨單。）

2. because of 「因為」
   ↳ My flight was canceled because of the strong wind.
   （因為強風的緣故，我的班機取消了。）

3. concerned 「擔心的，關心的」
   ↳ I'm really concerned about your health.
   （我實在很擔心你的健康狀況。）

4. pull out 「取出」
   ↳ Let me pull the file out of the drawer.
   （讓我從抽屜取出檔案。）

5. right here 「就在這」
   ↳ The document you are looking for is right here.
   （你在找的文件就在這兒。）

6. need you to... 「需要你…」
   ↳ I need you to help me translate this letter.
   （我要請你幫我翻譯這封信。）

7. make sure 「確定，確認」
   ↳ Will you make sure that the funds are transferred by Wednesday?
   （請你確認那筆錢會在禮拜三之前匯過來好嗎?）

8. get + 受詞 + 過去分詞 「使〜被…」

　↳ Will you get the wall repainted before the new tenant moves in?

　（可以請你在新房客搬進來之前將牆壁粉刷好嗎?）

9. needs 「需要，需求」

　↳ We must meet the educational needs of every child in town.

　（我們必須滿足鎮上每一位孩童在教育方面的需求。）

10. status 「狀態，狀況」

　↳ What's the status of the merger negotiation?

　（合併案的交涉狀況目前如何?）

實力測驗

你剛出差回來，秘書對你說在你出差期間有位女士到辦公室來找你，但並未留下姓名。請以三種不同的說法詢問秘書對那位女士有何印象。

參考解答　　1. Do you remember what she looked like?
　　　　　　2. I wonder if you remember what she looked like.
　　　　　　3. What did she look like? Can you remember?

| Chapter 7 | **The Blind Date** | 相親約會 |

Listening

Warm-up / Pre-questions

 請聽《Track 49》的新聞快報後回答下面問題。

新聞快報的內容是什麼?
(A) 現在的年輕人工作過於忙碌，連約會的時間都沒有了
(B) 在繁忙的生活型態下，年輕人尋找約會對象的方法改變了
(C) 在自由的生活型態下，現在的年輕人似乎比以前還有更多的機會約會

內容　Today's busy lifestyles have caused many young people to explore unconventional methods of finding dates.

中譯　今日繁忙的生活型態讓許多年輕人採取非傳統的方式尋找約會對象。

解答　(B)

解說　中文裡的「約會」通常是指「男女約定時間及地點見面之事」。不過英文的 date 除了上述的意思之外，還有「約會對象」、「日期」的意思，使用方法如 Are you coming with your date?（你會跟你的約會對象一起來嗎?）或 Let's set a date for the meeting.（我們決定一下會議的日期吧!）。在上述內文中，date 是指「約會對象」之意。此外，lifestyle 為「生活型態」、cause 為「使得，造成」、explore 為「探索」、unconventional 則為「不依慣例的」之意。

Listening Step 1

 請聽《Track 50》的會話後回答下面問題。

> 對話中的男女正在做什麼?
>   (A) 決定約會的日期
>   (B) 進行相親約會
>   (C) 勸朋友進行相親約會
>
> 解答   (B)

Listening Step 2

熟悉下列關鍵字

> nervous   緊張的,擔心的
> blind date   相親約會(原不相識的男女經由第三者的介紹而進行的初次約會)
> decide   決定
> disaster   徹底的失敗
> the Millers   米勒一家人
> alike   相似的,相像的
> neat freak   非常愛乾淨的人,有潔癖的人
> true   真的
> science fiction   科幻小說
> correct   正確的
> passion   熱情;熱愛之物
> biography   傳記
> fiction   小說
> spy story   偵探小說
> whodunit   推理小說(源自 Who done it? / Who did it?)

escape 逃脫；逃避的手段（方法）

seriousness 嚴肅，認真

accountant 會計師

room 空間，餘地

creativity 創造力

job 工作

engineer 工程師

bored 無聊，厭倦

appeal 吸引，引起興趣

1 請聽《Track 51》並在括弧內填入正確答案。

1. I was a little bit (　　　) about going on a blind date.

2. Just once and it was a (　　　)!

3. My (　　　) is reading biographies.

4. They are an (　　　) from all of the seriousness at work.

5. There is probably not much room for (　　　), is there?

解答

1. I was a little bit (nervous) about going on a blind date.

2. Just once and it was a (disaster)!

3. My (passion) is reading biographies.

4. They are an (escape) from all of the seriousness at work.

5. There is probably not much room for (creativity), is there?

1 請再聽一次《Track 50》的會話後回答下面問題。

1. 誰促成了這一次的相親約會？

(A) Janet

(B) 對話中的男士的友人

(C) Miller 一家人

2. 對話中的男士最喜歡讀什麼類別的書?

(A) 傳記

(B) 推理小說

(C) 科幻小說

解答   1. (C)   2. (A)

Listening Step 3

熟悉下列語句

a little bit　有一些
go on a blind date　參加相親約會
me, too　我也是
in common　有共通之處
make sense　有道理
black and white　黑白分明的
cut and dried　一板一眼的
get bored　感到無聊
here comes the waitress　女服務生過來了
figure out　想出; 決定

1 請聽《Track 52》並在括弧內填入正確答案。

1. I was (　　　) (　　　) (　　　) nervous about going on a blind date.

2. We had nothing (　　　) (　　　).

3. Everything is (　　　) (　　　) (　　　), cut and dried.

The Blind Date   **75**

4. There is always something new going on and I never ( ) ( ).

5. I guess we had better ( ) ( ) what we are going to order.

1 請再聽一次《Track 50》的會話後回答下面問題。

1. 兩個人的共通點是什麼?
   (A) 喜歡讀書
   (B) 喜歡看電影
   (C) 都在書店工作

2. Janet 對於閱讀推理小說有什麼看法?
   (A) 浪費時間
   (B) 可以豐富想像力
   (C) 可以從工作的緊張壓力中解放出來

3. 對話中的男士為什麼喜歡工程師的工作?
   (A) 薪水很高
   (B) 總是會有新的挑戰，不會感到厭倦
   (C) 工作的時間一定，而且有很長的年休

解答　　　　　　　　　　1. (A)　2. (C)　3. (B)

Speaking

會話

 請再聽一次《Track 50》。

Bill: Well, Janet, I have to tell you that I was a little bit nervous about going on a blind date, but I'm happy I decided to come.

Janet: Yes, me, too. I've never been on a blind date before. Have you?

Bill: Just once and it was a disaster! We had nothing in common.

Janet: The Millers seem to know us both really well and they kept telling me how much alike we are.

Bill: I know, they told me that too. They said that you were a "neat freak" too and that you could spend hours in a bookstore.

Janet: Both of those things are so true! Mr. Miller told me that you love to read science fiction. Is that correct?

Bill: I like science fiction, but my passion is reading biographies. I enjoy learning how famous people became who they are. What do you like to read?

Janet: I like to read fiction—spy stories and "whodunit" kind of books. They are an escape from all of the seriousness at work.

Bill: That makes sense. As an accountant there is probably not much room for creativity, is there?

Janet: No, not really. Everything is black and white, cut and dried. But I love my job. Are you happy with yours?

Bill: Yes. I really like being an engineer. There is always something new going on and I never get bored.

Janet: Oh, here comes the waitress. I guess we had better figure out what we are going to order. What on the menu appeals to you?

中　譯

比爾：珍娜，坦白說，在參加這次相親約會之前，我其實是有點緊張的。不過，我很高興最後我還是決定來了。

珍娜：是啊，我也有同感。我以前從來沒有參加過這種約會。你呢？

比爾：只參加過一次，不過那次實在是非常失敗。我們完全沒有共通之處。

珍娜：米勒一家人似乎蠻了解我們兩個人的，他們不斷提起我和你有多麼相似。

比爾：是啊，他們也是那麼告訴我的。他們說妳是一個「超級愛乾淨的人」，還說妳可以花很長的時間待在書店裡。

珍娜：他們說的都是真的！我聽米勒先生說你是個科幻小說迷，是真的嗎？

比爾：我是蠻喜歡閱讀科幻小說的，不過我真正的最愛還是傳記類。我非常喜歡研究名人的成功歷程。妳喜歡讀哪方面的書呢？

珍娜：我喜歡看小說，尤其是偵探和推理小說。它們能幫我暫時逃避嚴肅的工作。

比爾：有道理。當一個會計師恐怕沒有太多發揮想像力的空間吧？

珍娜：是沒有。所有的事情都是黑白分明，一板一眼的。不過，我熱愛我的工作。你滿意你的工作嗎？

比爾：滿意，我非常喜歡當一位工程師。工作上總是會有新的挑
　　　戰讓我不會感到厭煩。

珍娜：喔，女服務生過來了。我想我們還是先決定要點什麼東西
　　　吧。菜單上有沒有吸引你的食物呢？

語　法

● 口語說法的 me, too
　me, too 是「我也是」的口語說法，使用上非常普及，如 I was nervous
　too.，或是 I was happy too. 等都可以簡單地以 Me, too. 取代。

● enjoy 只能以動名詞作受詞
　enjoy 這個動詞只能以動名詞作受詞，例如 I enjoy learning how
　famous people became who they are. 的 learning 就是動名詞，而不用
　enjoy to ～。也就是說 I enjoy playing the piano. 是正確說法，而 I enjoy
　to play the piano. 則是錯誤的句子。這種只能以動名詞作受詞的動詞
　除了 enjoy 之外，還有 avoid（避免）、mind（介意）、quit（放棄）等。

● 修飾 something 的形容詞要放在後面
　修飾 something 的形容詞要像 something new（某樣新的東西）或是
　something old（某樣舊的東西）一樣，放在 something 的後面。此外，
　修飾 something 的不定詞也要放在 something 的後面，例如 something
　to eat（什麼可以吃的）或 something to drink（什麼可以喝的）。

Speaking Function 7

詢問「是否真是如此」、回答「正是如此」

請聽《Track 53》。

---

1. A: Jack told me you're going on a blind date this weekend. Is
　　that right?

B: Yes, that's right. I'm a little bit nervous already.

2. A: Is it true that Nancy is transferring to New York?

   B: Yes, that's true. She's leaving on Monday.

3. A: Are you giving away this stereo set?

   B: That's right.

解說

● 要詢問他人「那件事是真的嗎?」的時候,基本上有 Is that right? / Is that true? / Is that correct? 等三種說法。例如,當你想詢問對方是否真的要去和素未謀面的人約會,可以這樣問: I heard you're going on a blind date. Is that right?。若要語氣更為委婉些,可以用 Could you tell me if that's true? 或是 Would you mind telling me if that's correct? 的說法。

● Is it true that...? 也是詢問是否真是如此的講法,使用這個句型時,that 之後接續想要弄清楚的事情。例如,想要確認同事 Nancy 是否真的要調職到紐約時,可以這樣詢問: Is it true that Nancy is transferring to New York?,也可以把 true 換成 right 或是 correct,變成 Is it right that...? / Is it correct that...?。

● 要回答「沒錯,正是如此」,也有多種講法,其中最基本的回答方式就是: Yes, that's right.,此時當然也可以把 right 換成 true 或是 correct。若要像「你講的一點也沒錯」這樣加強說話的語氣時,則可以在 right 或 correct 之前加上 quite。另外,甚至可以只用 Exactly. 或 Absolutely. 等單一的副詞來回答,同樣也具有加強語氣的效果。

練習 1【代換】

 請隨《Track 54》做代換練習。

1. Tom told me that the meeting was put off till Thursday.
   Is that right?

   Is that true?
   Is that correct?
   Could you tell me if that's true?
   Would you mind telling me if that's correct?

2. Is it true *that Jack is going to China?*

   that the president is going to resign?
   that Jim is changing jobs again?
   that Mary is getting married?
   that you're going to Greece for vacation?

3. "Are you saying I have to have an operation?"
   "Yes, that's right."

   "Yes, that's quite right."
   "Yes, that's correct."
   "Yes, you're quite correct."
   "Yes, that's true."
   "Exactly."
   "Absolutely."

練習 2【角色扮演】

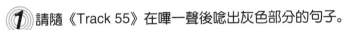 請隨《Track 55》在嗶一聲後唸出灰色部分的句子。

1. A: Mr. Atkinson told me you started taking scuba diving
   lessons. Is that right?

   B: Yes, that's right. It's quite fun.

2. A: Is it true that Nancy is coming back from New York?

   B: Yes, that's true. She's coming back on Wednesday.

3. A: Are you saying that I have to finish this report by Friday?

   B: That's right.

練習 3【覆誦重要語句】

1 請隨《Track 56》覆誦英文句子。

1. a little bit 「有一點」

   ↳ I'm a little bit upset.（我覺得有點煩。）

2. nervous about 「對～感到擔心」

   ↳ She's quite nervous about her driving test.

   （她很擔心她的駕照考試。）

3. go on a date 「約會」

   ↳ Mary and I are going on a date Friday night.

   （瑪莉與我在週五晚上有約會。）

4. in common 「有共通之處」

   ↳ I found that I had a lot in common with Mr. Keats.

   （我發現自己和濟慈先生有許多共通之處。）

5. keep doing 「不斷做」

   ↳ He kept saying I wasn't what he expected.

   （他不停地說我和他想像中的不一樣。）

6. spend hours 「花費長時間」

   ↳ He spent hours surfing the net.（他長時間在上網。）

7. passion 「熱情；熱愛之物」

   ↳ Expensive clothes and jewels are her passion.

   （她的最愛是昂貴的衣服與珠寶。）

8. room 「空間；餘地」

　↳I'm afraid there's little room for creativity in my kind of work. (我這類的工作恐怕不太有發揮創造力的空間。)

9. black and white 「黑白分明的」

　↳Things are not always black and white.

　(事情不是永遠都是黑白分明的。)

10. figure out 「想出；理解」

　↳It took me days to figure out a solution to the problem. (我花了好幾天的時間才想出那個問題的解決辦法。)

實力測驗

意外聽見你經常光顧的餐廳即將結束營業的消息，你想確定事情的真假。請用三種不同的說法詢問店長這件事。

參考解答
1. I heard you're closing down. Is that right?
2. I heard you're closing down. Is that correct?
3. I heard you're closing down. Is that true?

The Transfer 調 職

Listening

Warm-up / Pre-questions

 請聽《Track 57》的新聞快報後回答下面問題。

新聞快報的內容是什麼?

(A) Matrix 公司打算向東擴展事業版圖

(B) Matrix 公司打算在南加州發展

(C) Matrix 公司打算將總公司移到德州的達拉斯市

內容　Matrix, Inc., the Southern California wireless communication giant, will be expanding its network east, opening a new facility in Dallas, Texas early next month.

中譯　南加州的無線通訊大廠 Matrix 公司,將於下個月月初在德州達拉斯市設立新的營業機構,以便向東擴展其行銷網。

解答　(A)

解說　will be expanding 是未來進行式,用以表示「未來計畫採取的行動」。Inc. 是 incorporated(公司組織的)的縮略,接於公司名之後。wireless communication 為「無線通訊」、giant 為「大型廠商」、expand 為「擴大」、network 在此指「成網狀分布的企業營運系統」、facility 為「設施,機構」之意。

Listening Step 1

請聽《Track 58》的會話後回答下面問題。

James 在擔心什麼事?

  (A) 被降級

  (B) 銷售成績不佳

  (C) 被調職

解答   (C)

Listening Step 2

熟悉下列關鍵字

payroll budget proposal 薪資預算提案

hire 雇,請

facility coordinator 使機構運作順利的協調人員

hate 憎恨,討厭

transfer 調職,轉任

prospective 預期的,盼望中的

transferee 被調職的人

CEO= Chief Executive Officer 公司最高決策者,總裁

mention 提及,說到

board meeting 董事會議

last-minute 最後一分鐘的,倉促的

arrangement 安排

guess 推測,猜想

discuss 討論

appreciate 感激,感謝

run 經營,運作

smoothly 順利地

1 請聽《Track 59》並在括弧內填入正確答案。

1. It looks like they are going to (　　　　) about 300 new technicians.
2. It looks like we will be (　　　　) four of ours to Texas for a year.
3. Your name came up yesterday as a (　　　　) transferee.
4. He (　　　　) it in the board meeting yesterday.
5. I would (　　　　) it if you don't mention I told you first.

解答

1. It looks like they are going to (hire) about 300 new technicians.
2. It looks like we will be (transferring) four of ours to Texas for a year.
3. Your name came up yesterday as a (prospective) transferee.
4. He (mentioned) it in the board meeting yesterday.
5. I would (appreciate) it if you don't mention I told you first.

1 請再聽一次《Track 58》的會話後回答下面問題。

1. David 剛做完什麼事?
   (A) 剛開完會
   (B) 剛整理完出差報告
   (C) 剛完成薪資預算案
2. 有幾個人將會被調職?
   (A) 4 人
   (B) 30 人
   (C) 300 人

解答　　　　　　　　　　　　　　　　1. (C)　　2. (A)

Listening Step 3

熟悉下列語句

---

come along　進行
look like　看起來似乎
What about ～?　關於～如何?
up and running　正常營運的，上軌道的
come up　(話題等在談話、會議中)被提到
This is nothing to joke about.　這可不是開玩笑的。
set up　建立，設立
call in　叫進來
I would appreciate it if you...　假如你…我會很感激。
way around　規避～的方法
get called into　被叫進去

---

1 請聽《Track 60》並在括弧內填入正確答案。

1. How is that (　　) (　　)?
2. The new facility is (　　) (　　) (　　).
3. This is nothing (　　) (　　) (　　).
4. I'd (　　) (　　) (　　) you don't mention I told you first.
5. Is there any (　　) (　　) my being transferred?

解答

1. How is that (coming) (along)?
2. The new facility is (up) (and) (running).
3. This is nothing (to) (joke) (about).
4. I'd (appreciate) (it) (if) you don't mention I told you first.
5. Is there any (way) (around) my being transferred?

請再聽一次《Track 58》的會話後回答下面問題。

1. James 將擔任什麼職務？
   (A) 會計師
   (B) 重要幹部
   (C) 機構協調人員
2. James 明天會跟誰談事情？
   (A) David
   (B) Mr. Parker
   (C) 達拉斯分公司的總經理
3. James 在明天的會談之前會先做什麼？
   (A) 好好想一想
   (B) 跟上司商量
   (C) 先詳細調查一下新機構的事

解答	1. (C)　2. (B)　3. (A)

Speaking

會話

請再聽一次《Track 58》。

James: Hi, David. How are you doing?

David: Pretty good, James. I'm just finishing this payroll budget proposal for the opening of the new facility next month.

James: How is that coming along? How many new people will they be hiring?

David: It looks like they are going to hire about 300 new technicians and 30 new managers.

James: What about facility coordinators?

David: I hate to tell you this, James, but it looks like we will be transferring four of ours to Texas for a year until the new facility is up and running. Your name came up yesterday as a prospective transferee.

James: Are you sure about that, David? This is nothing to joke about. You know I don't want to move to Texas.

David: I'm pretty certain that the CEO wants you, Roger, Daniel, and Eliot to go and get the shop set up. He mentioned it in the board meeting yesterday.

James: Nobody has said anything to me yet. This is really a last-minute kind of arrangement.

David: I know. I'm guessing that Mr. Parker will be calling you in today or tomorrow to discuss it. I'd appreciate it if you don't mention I told you first.

James: Of course I won't, but is there any way around my being transferred?

David: You might be able to get back here in six months if the four of you can get things running smoothly and the managers trained quickly.

James: This is all a really big shock. I have some thinking to do before I get called into that meeting.

詹姆士：嗨，大衛，最近好嗎?

大　衛：還不賴，詹姆士。我才剛為下個月要開始營運的新機構完成了所有員工的薪資預算提案。

詹姆士：提案進行得如何? 公司將會雇用多少名新進員工?

大　衛：看來大約會新增加三百名技術師和三十名管理人員。

詹姆士：那關於使新機構運作順利的協調人員呢?

大　衛：詹姆士，我真不想對你提起這件事。不過，看樣子我們這裡似乎得調派四位人員到德州一年，直到新機構的營運完全上軌道為止。你是昨天被提到的人選之一。

詹姆士：大衛，你確定這是真的嗎? 這可不是開玩笑的，你知道我不想搬去德州。

大　衛：我蠻肯定總裁希望是由你、羅傑、丹尼爾，和艾略特四個人去把那裡的業務建立起來。這是他昨天在董事會議上親口說的。

詹姆士：根本沒有人跟我提起這件事。這一定是倉促之下所做的安排。

大　衛：我知道。不過我猜想派克先生今天或明天一定會打電話跟你討論這件事。如果你能別提起我事先有告訴過你，我會很感激的。

詹姆士：這當然，我不會說出來。不過有沒有辦法能讓我不被調職呢?

大　衛：假如你們四個人能在半年內讓一切運作順利並完成管理人員的訓練，就有可能被調回來。

詹姆士：這真是一大打擊。在被叫去開會之前，我得先好好想清楚了。

- 被動語態的動名詞

  要讓動名詞帶有「被～」的語意時，可以用 being 加動詞的過去分詞來表示。例如 Of course I won't, but is there any way around my being transferred? 的句子中，my being transferred 就是指「我被調職」這件事。整句話的意思相當於 Is it possible to avoid my being transferred?；而若改成 I must avoid being transferred to Texas. 則語氣更為強烈。

- might 用以表示對未來的事不確定的推測

  may 的過去式 might 可用以表示對於未來的事不確定的推測。例如對於這樣的問句：Are you going to the party? (你會去參加派對嗎?)，當你還沒決定去或不去時，可以回答 I might, I might not.。而會話內容中 You *might* be able to get back here in six months. 則是「或許六個月後你就能回到這裡」的推測說法。

- 表示強調的 all

  This is *all* a really big shock. 中的 all 當作副詞，用以加強語氣。I'm *all* confused. (我都被搞昏頭了) 和 He's *all* against my proposal. (他完全反對我的計畫) 這兩句話中，all 也是用來表示強調之意。

Speaking Function 8

「看起來好像⋯」「似乎可能⋯」

 請聽《Track 61》。

1. A: It looks like they are going to transfer you to Dallas.

   B: No kidding. I just bought a new house here a month ago.

2. A: How much do you think this project will cost?

   B: Probably at least half a million dollars.

3. A: I really don't know where I lost my passport.

   B: It's possible that you lost it in the theater.

練習 1【代換】

請隨《Track 62》做代換練習。

   1. *It looks like it's going to*   rain this afternoon.

   It looks as if it might
   It looks like
   It seems like it's going to
   It seems as if it might
   It seems like

2. "Will you be going to Miami with Mr. Hudson?"
   "*Probably, I will.*"
   "Maybe, but I'm not sure."
   "Perhaps, I will."
   "Possibly. I'm not sure yet."

3. *It's quite possible* that all new staff will be employed on a
   part-time basis.

   It's quite probable
   It's quite likely
   It's not unlikely

練習 2【角色扮演】

 請隨《Track 63》在嗶一聲後唸出灰色部分的句子。

1. A: We haven't heard from Mr. Brown of ST Communica-
      tions for weeks.
   B: It looks like we won't be able to make a deal with his
      company.
2. A: How come Linda is late?
   B: Probably she is caught in the traffic jam.
3. A: I don't understand why we haven't received the new
      catalog yet.
   B: It's quite possible that they might have forgotten to mail it
      to us.

練習 3【覆誦重要語句】

① 請隨《Track 64》覆誦英文句子。

1. come along 「進行」
   ↳ How was your new project coming along?
   （你的新計畫進展得如何？）

2. I hate to tell you this, but... 「我真不想對你提起，不過…」
   ↳ I hate to tell you this, but we have to cut your salary by 10% starting next month.（我真不想對你提起，不過下個月起你的薪水必須調降百分之十。）

3. up and running 「正常營運的，上軌道的」
   ↳ Will you manage the new store in Carmel until it is up and running?
   （你能不能將卡莫新開張的那家商店經營到上軌道為止？）

4. come up 「（話題等）被提到」
   ↳ Your name came up at the promotion meeting yesterday.
   （在昨天的升遷會議上有提到你的名字。）

5. set up 「建立，設立」
   ↳ It won't be an easy job to set up a new branch in San Francisco.
   （要在舊金山開設一家新分公司不是一件容易的事。）

6. last-minute 「最後一分鐘的，倉促的」
   ↳ They made last-minute changes to the contract.
   （他們在最後一分鐘更改了合約。）

7. I'd appreciate it if... 「假如你…我會很感激。」
   ↳ I'd appreciate it very much if you keep it secret.
   （假如你能保密，我會很感激。）

8. way around 「規避～的方法」

　　↳Is there any way around having an operation for this sickness?（治療這種疾病可不可以不開刀？）

9. run smoothly 「進行順利」

　　↳I just want to make sure everything runs smoothly and on time.（我只是要確認一切都能如期順利進行。）

10. have some thinking to do 「好好思索一番」

　　↳I have some thinking to do before I make a decision.（在下決定之前，我必須好好思索一番。）

實力測驗

在廣告公司工作的你，約在兩個星期前接到客戶想要製作新廣告的委託，但是對於廣告的規模以及廣告的訴求一直無法取得共識。最近，客戶方面似乎有讓步的意思，可望在下週有結果。剛好這時候，上司來問你這件廣告案進行得如何？請你用三種說法回答。

參考解答

1. It looks like we'll be able to close the deal sometime next week.

2. Probably we'll be able to close the deal sometime next week.

3. It's quite likely that we'll be able to close the deal sometime next week.

Female Executive 女性主管

Listening

Warm-up / Pre-questions

 請聽《Track 1》的新聞快報後回答下面問題。

Linda Sherman 得到了什麼獎?

(A) 中小企業年度風雲人物獎

(B) 年度最爛服裝獎

(C) 年度最佳女性投資人獎

內容　Small Business Administration honors Linda Sherman with the "Small Business Person of the Year Award."

中譯　琳達・雪曼榮獲中小企業管理局頒發「中小企業年度風雲人物獎」。

解答　(A)

解說　電視或廣播中,處理每一條新聞標題的方式和報紙是一樣的,雖然描述的是過去已經發生的事,但在習慣上仍會用現在式。所以上述例句: Small Business Administration honors...,雖然敘述的是已經發生的事實,當中的動詞還是用第三人稱單數的 honors。此外,Small Business Administration 為「中小企業管理局」、honor 為「給予榮耀」、award 為「獎項」之意。

Listening Step 1

②請聽《Track 2》的會話後回答下面問題。

對話中的兩位女士在談論誰?

(A) 新任的女總經理

(B) 高中時代的朋友

(C) 世界知名的電腦程式設計師

解答 (B)

Listening Step 2

熟悉下列關鍵字

---

leading article　頭條新聞

section　（報紙的）版, 欄

paper　報紙

reunion　同學會

award　獎

own　擁有

business　事業, 企業

create　創立

enable　使可能

monitor　監視

control　控制, 掌管

employee　職員

bright　聰明的

business minded　有商業頭腦的

math　數學

imagine　想像

"people" person　善於與人相處的人

---

run　經營
face-to-face　面對面的，直接的
interaction　交流，互動
congratulate　恭喜

②請聽《Track 3》並在括弧內填入正確答案。

1. The leading (　　) for the business section was about our old friend from high school.
2. She was given an (　　) from the Small Business Administration.
3. She (　　) a company.
4. I always felt that Linda was incredibly (　　) and business minded.
5. I just never (　　) her as a "people" person running a company.

解答

1. The leading (article) for the business section was about our old friend from high school.
2. She was given an (award) from the Small Business Administration.
3. She (created) a company.
4. I always felt that Linda was incredibly (bright) and business minded.
5. I just never (imagined) her as a "people" person running a company.

②請再聽一次《Track 2》的會話後回答下面問題。

1. Linda Sherman 經營什麼公司？
 (A) 保全公司

(B) 與電腦相關的雜誌出版社

(C) 研發套裝軟體的電腦公司

2. 除了資訊科學之外，Linda Sherman 還擅長什麼科目？

(A) 數學

(B) 化學

(C) 物理

解答   1. (C)   2. (A)

Listening Step 3

熟悉下列語句

You bet!　當然! 的確!
in the paper　在報紙上，上報紙
lose track of　與～失去聯絡
That's something.　那真是了不起。
to be honest with you　坦白說，不瞞你說

② 請聽《Track 4》並在括弧內填入正確答案。

1. (　　) (　　　) you did!

2. Why was she (　　) (　　) (　　) ?

3. I (　　) (　　) (　　　) her since our 10-year high school reunion.

4. (　　) (　　　).

5. Well, to be quite (　　) (　　) (　　), Jessica, I always felt that Linda was incredibly bright and business minded.

解答

1. (You) (bet) you did!
2. Why was she (in) (the) (paper)?
3. I (lost) (track) (of) her since our 10-year high school reunion.
4. (That's) (something).
5. Well, to be quite (honest) (with) (you), Jessica, I always felt that Linda was incredibly bright and business minded.

② 請再聽一次《Track 2》的會話後回答下面問題。

1. Linda Sherman 為什麼會上報?
   (A) 因為她是中小企業的第一位女總經理
   (B) 因為她寫了一篇有關中小企業經營的報導
   (C) 因為她榮獲中小企業年度風雲人物獎

2. Jessica 跟 Linda Sherman 之間的關係如何?
   (A) 彼此很久沒聯絡了
   (B) 互相常以 e-mail 聯絡
   (C) 偶而一起吃吃飯

3. 從兩人的對話中,你對 Linda Sherman 有什麼印象?
   (A) 她是個外向且健談的人
   (B) 她是個不太善於與人交際的人
   (C) 她是個具有領導能力的人

解答   1. (C)   2. (A)   3. (B)

Speaking

會話

 請再聽一次《Track 2》。

Emily: Jessica, did you see today's newspaper?

Jessica: No, I haven't had the chance to look at it. Did I miss something important?

Emily: You bet you did! The leading article for the business section was about our old friend from high school—Linda Sherman.

Jessica: You're kidding! Why was she in the paper? I've lost track of her since our 10-year high school reunion.

Emily: She was given an award from the Small Business Administration for being the Small Business Person of the Year.

Jessica: That's something. I didn't even know she owned a business!

Emily: She created a company that makes software that enables other companies to monitor and control how their employees use the Internet.

Jessica: That's unbelievable! I would never have guessed that someone like Linda Sherman could do something like that.

Emily: Well, to be quite honest with you, Jessica, I always felt that Linda was incredibly bright and business minded.

Jessica: You know, she was really good at math and computer science, but I just never imagined her as a "people" person running a company.

Emily: Well, She works with computers so she might not have a lot of face-to-face interaction with other people and she probably has someone doing her marketing for her.

Jessica: That makes sense. Well, I think we should give her a call or send her an e-mail to congratulate her. Do you think she'll remember us?

Emily: I guess we'll find out. Let's call her tomorrow.

中　譯 ···

愛蜜麗：潔西卡，妳看了今天的報紙嗎？

潔西卡：沒有，我還沒有機會看。我錯過了什麼重要新聞嗎？

愛蜜麗：妳的確錯過了！工商版的頭條講的是我們高中的老同學 ──琳達‧雪曼。

潔西卡：妳在開玩笑吧！她怎麼會上報紙呢？自從我們十週年的 高中同學會後，我就和她失去聯絡了。

愛蜜麗：她得了中小企業管理局所頒發的「中小企業年度風雲人 物獎」。

潔西卡：這真是了不起。我甚至不知道她已經擁有自己的公司了。

愛蜜麗：她創立了一家公司，研發讓其他企業能監看並控管員工 使用網路的軟體。

潔西卡：這真是令人難以相信！我從來沒想到像琳達‧雪曼那樣 的人會有如此成就。

愛蜜麗：潔西卡，不瞞妳說，我一直認為琳達不但聰明絕頂而且 有商業頭腦。

潔西卡：是啊，她在數學與資訊科學方面非常拿手，不過我從來
　　　　沒想過她會是個善於與人相處的企業經營者。

愛蜜麗：喔，她的工作與電腦有關，所以可能跟其他人不會有很
　　　　多面對面的互動，而且她應該有請專人來替她處理行銷
　　　　的業務。

潔西卡：那樣就說得通了。我想我們應該打通電話或是發封電子
　　　　郵件恭喜她。妳認為她會記得我們嗎？

愛蜜麗：到時候就知道了。明天撥通電話給她吧!

語　法 ....

● 表示「公司」之意的 business
  business 除了表示「商業」之外，也有「公司」、「商店」之意。表示
  此意時，視作可數名詞，前面要加不定冠詞 a，例如：own a business
  （擁有一家公司）/ run a business（經營一家公司）/ open a business（開
  業）/ close a business（結束營業）。

● 以 would have + 過去分詞構成的委婉表達方式
  would have + 過去分詞（表示過去的假設語氣）可作為委婉的表達方
  式，I would have never guessed... 為「我從來沒想過…」，此時也可如
  同會話句，將 never 置於 have 之前，加強助動詞 have。其他例句如：
  Who would have thought such a thing?（誰會想到這樣的事?）。

Speaking Function 9

講述意見或無意見的說法

 請聽《Track 5》。

1. A: Who do you recommend for the position of sales manager?
   B: I think Cathy is a good candidate for the position.

2. A: What do you think about the itinerary?

   B: I think it's well planned.

3. A: What do you think about the acquisition scheme?

   B: I really don't know what to say about it.

解說

● 講述意見的最簡單的表達方式是以 I think 開頭，接著說明所持的意見。think 也可以用 believe/suppose/feel/consider 等字替換。believe 給人的感覺比 think 語氣更強烈、相信的程度更深，是會話中經常使用到的單字，suppose 通常用於判斷的根據較為薄弱的情況下，feel 則是比 think 更語帶保留的說法，consider 則用於已經經過深思熟慮或是依經驗判斷的情況下。

● 在講述意見時，也可以像 In my opinion,...（就我看來…）這樣，以介系詞片語來開啟話頭。類似的說法還有 In my view,... 以及 From my point of view,... 等。其他例如 As I see it / As far as I'm concerned 也可以用於句首來表示自己的意見，其意義相當於中文裡的「以我之見」、「就我所知」。

● 詢問他人意見時，最基本的表達方式為 What do you think about ～?；此處的 about 可以用 of 替換，改成 What do you think of ～?。另外可以使用 opinion 這個字，說成 What's your opinion of ～?，或是用 view/feeling 造句，改說：What are your views on ～? / What are your feelings about ～?。

● 對於他人的詢問沒什麼意見時，可以用 I really don't know what to say about ～，或者用 think 取代 say，變成 I really don't know what to think about ～。另外，可以使用 opinion 或 feeling，說成 I really don't have any opinion about ～ / I have no strong feelings about ～。若是對一件事沒有什麼特別看法時，可以說 I can't say I have any particular views on ～。

練習 1 【代換】

②請隨《Track 6》做代換練習。

1. *I think* it's a very good business opportunity.
   I believe
   I suppose
   I feel
   I consider

2. *In my opinion,* the discount rate is reasonable.
   In my view,
   From my point of view,
   As I see it,
   As far as I'm concerned,

3. *What do you think about* the new catalog?
   What do you think of
   What's your opinion of
   What are your views on
   What are your feelings about

4. *I really don't know what to say about* the merger proposal.

   I really don't know what to think about
   I really don't have any opinion about
   I have no strong feelings about
   I can't say I have any particular views on

練習 2【角色扮演】

 請隨《Track 7》在嗶一聲後唸出灰色部分的句子。

1. A: What do you think of the price?

   B: I think it's reasonable.

2. A: What do you think about his plan?

   B: I don't think it's economically feasible.

3. A: What do you think of the plan to buy new computer equipment?

   B: I really don't know what to say about it.

練習 3【覆誦重要語句】

 請隨《Track 8》覆誦英文句子。

1. I haven't had the chance to 「我還沒有機會，我還來不及」

   ↳ I haven't had the chance to check my e-mail.

   （我還來不及檢查我的電子郵件信箱。）

2. miss 「錯過」

   ↳ Everybody except Tom missed the subtle joke.

   （除了湯姆，所有的人都沒留意到這則絕妙笑話。）

3. in the paper 「在報紙上」

   ↳ I saw the ad in the paper.（我在報紙上看見這則廣告。）

4. lose track of 「與～失去聯絡」

   ↳ I lost track of all the project members.

   （我和這個研究計畫的所有成員都失去了聯絡。）

5. a business 「公司，事業」

   ↳ He is looking forward to establishing a business with his

retirement allowance.

（他期待能用退休金來建立自己的事業。）

6. monitor 「監看，監視」

↳ Bankers monitor cash flow on the computer.

（銀行業者盯著電腦螢幕上的現金流量。）

7. I would have never guessed that... 「我從來沒想過…」

↳ I would have never guessed that Jim would become a pro basketball player.

（我從來沒想過吉姆會成為職業籃球員。）

8. to be honest with you 「坦白說，不瞞你說」

↳ To be honest with you, I'm not very happy with your performance. （坦白說，我對你的表現不是很滿意。）

9. I always felt that... 「我一直認為…」

↳ I always felt that Jack was too self-centered and aggressive.

（我一直認為傑克太過於自我中心而且蠻幹好強。）

10. imagine ～ as... 「想像～是…」

↳ I haven't met her, but I imagine her as a bright and business minded person. （我從沒見過她，不過我想她是個聰明而且有商業頭腦的人。）

實力測驗

經理徵詢你對於新商品目錄上樣本的意見，你要怎麼回答呢？請試著以三種不同的說法回答看看。

參考解答	1. I think it's very good. Excellent, in fact.
	2. I believe it's excellent, one of the best we've made.
	3. As I see it, it needs to be refined.

Promotion 晉　昇

Listening

Warm-up / Pre-questions

 請聽《Track 9》的新聞快報後回答下面問題。

Union Carbon 公司對 Jack Johnson 做了什麼?
(A) 讚揚他的功勞
(B) 不讓他晉昇
(C) 讓他榮昇

內容　In an award ceremony today, Union Carbon Inc. honored Jack Johnson as he embarks on his new role as the company's Corporate Financial Officer.

中譯　Union Carbon 公司今天在一項頒獎典禮中，宣布傑克・強森將晉昇為公司高級財務主管。

解答　(C)

解說　在上面的句子中，前面的 as 為連接詞，語意與 while 相同；後面的 as 則是介系詞，為「作為～」之意。此外，award ceremony 為「頒獎典禮」、honor 為「給予榮耀」、embark 為「開始從事」、role 為「任務，職務」、Corporate Financial Officer 為「公司高級財務主管」之意。

Listening Step 1

 請聽《Track 10》的會話後回答下面問題。

> Mark 打電話到哪裡找 Jack？
>
> (A) Jack 的辦公室
>
> (B) Jack 的家裡
>
> (C) Jack 出差的地方
>
> 解答   (A)

Listening Step 2

熟悉下列關鍵字

> a quick call   簡短的電話
>
> congratulations   恭喜，祝賀
>
> pleased   高興的，愉悅的
>
> promotion   升職
>
> respect   尊敬，尊重
>
> soul   靈魂
>
> reward   *v.* 回報；*n.* 報酬
>
> prime   最佳的
>
> location   地點，位置
>
> face   面對
>
> hardly   幾乎不
>
> funny   好笑的，可笑的
>
> deserve   值得
>
> celebrate   慶祝

 請聽《Track 11》並在括弧內填入正確答案。

    1. I just wanted to tell you (   ) on your new position.

2. I'm really pleased with the (　　　).

3. I have nothing but (　　　) for you.

4. Speaking of (　　　), where is your new office?

5. You really (　　　) the job.

解答

1. I just wanted to tell you (congratulations) on your new position.

2. I'm really pleased with the (promotion).

3. I have nothing but (respect) for you.

4. Speaking of (rewards), where is your new office?

5. You really (deserve) the job.

② 請再聽一次《Track 10》的會話後回答下面問題。

1. Jack 與 Mark 的關係為何?

　(A) 雇用者與被雇用者

　(B) 同事

　(C) 上司與部屬

2. Jack 的新辦公室在哪裡?

　(A) 現在的辦公大樓的頂樓

　(B) 新大樓景觀最好的地方

　(C) 5 樓景觀最好的地方

解答　　　　　　　　　　　　　　　1. (B)　2. (C)

Listening Step 3

熟悉下列語句

make it to the top　使成功

nothing but 除了~之外沒有別的
give one's heart and soul 全心全意地付出
for the last 10 years 過去這十年來
speaking of 談到
can hardly wait 幾乎等不及
stop by 順道拜訪
any time you like 隨時
go to one's head 使~眩暈，使~沖昏頭
How about if... …如何？

②請聽《Track 12》並在括弧內填入正確答案。

1. I know how hard you've worked to (　　) (　　) to the top.

2. I know both of us have given our (　　) (　　) (　　) to this company for the last 10 years.

3. I (　　) (　　) (　　) to move into it.

4. Well, Mark, (　　) (　　) any time you like.

5. The position is already (　　) (　　) (　　) (　　).

解答

1. I know how hard you've worked to (make) (it) to the top.

2. I know both of us have given our (hearts) (and) (souls) to this company for the last 10 years.

3. I (can) (hardly) (wait) to move into it.

4. Well, Mark, (stop) (by) any time you like.

5. The position is already (going) (to) (your) (head).

②請再聽一次《Track 10》的會話後回答下面問題。

1. Mark 對 Jack 抱持著怎樣的態度？
　(A) 尊敬他
　(B) 把他看成競爭對手
　(C) 認為他是值得信賴的同事

2. Jack 覺得新辦公室怎麼樣？
　(A) 覺得太大了
　(B) 有兩扇窗戶，令人難以定下心來
　(C) 想早一點搬進去

3. 在對話的最後，Mark 提議做什麼？
　(A) 一起去喝酒慶祝
　(B) 去看看新辦公室
　(C) 請 Jack 傳授成功的秘訣

解答　　　　　　　　　　　1. (A)　　2. (C)　　3. (A)

Speaking

會話

 請再聽一次《Track 10》。

Mark: Hi, Jack. I just wanted to give you a quick call and tell you congratulations on your new position.

Jack: Thanks, Mark. I'm really pleased with the promotion.

Mark: Well, Jack, I know how hard you've worked to make it to the top and I have nothing but respect for you.

Jack: Thanks, Mark. That really means a lot to me. I know both of us have given our hearts and souls to this company for the last 10 years and it's nice to finally be rewarded.

Mark: Speaking of rewards, where is your new office?

Jack: I'm glad you asked. It's in a prime location on the 5th floor with south and west facing windows. I can hardly wait to move into it.

Mark: You're one lucky man. I wish I had an office like that!

Jack: Well, Mark, stop by any time you like. You can sit at my desk to see what it feels like.

Mark: That's pretty funny, Jack. The position is already going to your head.

Jack: Come on, Mark, you know I'm just kidding.

Mark: Yes, I know. You really deserve the job. How about if we stop after work today for a drink to celebrate?

Jack: That sounds great. Let's meet at the Oak Bar at 6 o'clock.

Mark: All right. See you then.

中　譯 ....

馬克：嗨，傑克，我打這通電話只是想說聲恭喜你升官了。

傑克：馬克，謝謝。對於這次能獲得晉昇我實在很高興。

馬克：是啊，傑克，我很清楚你為了這次升職付出很大的努力，對你我只有敬佩二字可言。

傑克：馬克，謝謝。這對我實在意義非凡。我們兩個在過去這十年來對公司全心全意地付出，現在能有回報真好。

馬克：談到回報，你的新辦公室在哪？

傑克：問得好！我的新辦公室將會在五樓的最佳位置，有面向西

邊與南邊的窗戶。我已經等不及要搬過去了。

馬克： 你真是個幸運的傢伙！我真希望也有像那樣的辦公室！

傑克： 馬克，隨時歡迎你過來參觀，你可以坐在我的位置上好好感受一下。

馬克： 那很可笑，傑克。看來升官把你給沖昏頭了。

傑克： 別認真，馬克，你也知道我只是在開玩笑。

馬克： 好，我知道。這個職位的確是你應得的。我們今天下班後去喝兩杯慶祝一下如何？

傑克： 好主意！那我們六點在橡木酒吧碰面。

馬克： 沒問題，到時候見囉！

語　法

● 表示「祝賀」之意的 congratulations
要表達「恭喜！」之意時，通常都是用複數形 Congratulations! 表達。
若要表示「恭喜升官」，則須與介系詞 on 連用，說成 Congratulations
on your promotion.。

● 用以表示否定的副詞
帶有否定意味的副詞除了 hardly 之外，還有 scarcely、barely 等。若
要表達「幾乎不～」，hardly 是最普遍使用的用語，scarcely 則稍帶正
式、生硬的感覺。barely 的否定意味最弱，帶有「勉勉強強，好不容
易才～」的語意，肯定意味較濃厚。例句如：I can *hardly* believe it.（我
幾乎無法相信）/ There's *scarcely* any milk left.（牛奶幾乎一滴不剩）/
I could *barely* hear his voice.（我好不容易才聽見他的聲音）。

● 使用 wish 的假設語氣
「I wish + 主詞 + 過去式」可用以表示現在無法實現的願望。例如：
I wish I were a bird.（我希望我是一隻鳥），或是 I wish I could speak
English as an English native speaker.（我希望我的英語能說得像以英文
為母語的人那樣好）。

Speaking Function 10

② 請聽《Track 13》。

---

1. A: Congratulations on your promotion.

   B: Thank you. I'm really pleased with the promotion.

2. A: Your proposal was accepted.

   B: That's great!

3. A: I just wanted to call and congratulate you on your promotion.

   B: Thank you. I can't say how pleased I am about the promotion.

解說

● 要表達喜悅或滿足的心情，可以用 pleased 或是 delighted 等形容詞，例如 I'm really pleased., 也可以複雜一點與介系詞 with, about, at, by 等連用，表達對某件事情感到高興。with 是一般最常使用的說法，about 是對事物，at 接續所見所聞的事，by 則接續人的行為。有時候也可以接續 to 引導的不定詞，例如: We're very pleased to hear that. (聽到這個消息令我們很高興)。

● 另外，可以用 That's ～ 的句型來表示喜悅或滿足，That's 的後面可接續 great, terrific, fantastic, super, awesome 等形容詞，表示看到、得知這件事「真是太棒了！」。或者也可以用感嘆的語氣說: Great! / Terrific! / Fantastic! / Super! / Awesome!，雖然只有一個字，也能傳遞高興的感覺。

● I can't say how pleased I am... 雖然是稍帶正式的說法，卻也是一種強調喜悅之情的語句。除了 pleased 之外，可以用 delighted, satisfied, contented (滿足的), gratified (滿意的) 等字加以取代。

練習 1【代換】

2 請隨《Track 14》做代換練習。

1. *I'm pleased with*   the promotion.
   I'm delighted with
   I'm satisfied with
   I'm contented with
   I'm gratified with

2. That's *great*!
   terrific!
   fantastic!
   super!
   awesome!

3. *I can't say how pleased I am*   about the award.
   I can't say how delighted I am
   I can't say how happy I am
   I can't say how glad I am
   I can't say how satisfied I am

練習 2【角色扮演】

2 請隨《Track 15》在嗶一聲後唸出灰色部分的句子。

1. A: Congratulations! You've passed your exam.
   B: Thank you. I'm really pleased with the result.

2. A: You've got the position.
   B: That's great!

3. A: Your application for the grant was approved.

B: Great! I can't say how pleased I am about the grant.

練習 3【覆誦重要語句】

②請隨《Track 16》覆誦英文句子。

1. congratulations 「恭喜，祝賀」

↳Congratulations on passing the entrance examination!
（恭喜你通過入學考試!）

2. make it to the top 「使成功」

↳If you put your mind to it, you can make it to the top.
（只要你肯用心，就一定會成功。）

3. nothing but 「除了～之外沒有別的」

↳He wanted nothing but respect from his colleagues.
（他除了希望得到同事的尊敬之外，其他別無所求。）

4. give one's heart and soul 「全心全意地付出」

↳He has given his heart and soul to his research on
superconductivity. （他專心致力於超導方面的研究。）

5. speaking of 「談到」

↳Speaking of the vacation, has Tom come back from his
vacation in Switzerland?
（談到假期，湯姆從瑞士度假回來了嗎?）

6. hardly 「幾乎不」

↳I can hardly wait to go to Turkey for my vacation.
（我幾乎等不及要去土耳其度假了。）

7. stop by 「順道拜訪」

↳I stopped by Mike's office on my way home.

（我回家的途中到馬克的辦公室停留了一下。）

8. any time you like 「隨時」

    ↳ You can stop me and ask a question any time you like.

    （你可以隨時打斷我並提出問題。）

9. go to one's head 「使～眩暈，使～沖昏頭」

    ↳ The success of the deal is really going to his head.

    （順利完成那筆交易的喜悅沖昏了他的頭。）

10. how about if... 「…如何?」

    ↳ How about if we dine out tonight?

    （我們今晚外出用餐如何?）

實力測驗

你好不容易結束了三年獨自調任外地的生活，現在終於可以回總公司服務，聽到這個消息的友人紛紛向你道賀，請試著以三種不同的說法向友人表達你高興的心情。

參考解答

1. I'm really pleased with my going back to the head office.

2. I'm really delighted with my going back to the head office.

3. I can't say how pleased I am about my going back to the head office.

| Renting an Apartment | 租公寓 |

Listening

Warm-up / Pre-questions

 請聽《Track 17》的新聞快報後回答下面問題。

從新聞快報中瞭解到什麼事情?
 (A) 到西雅圖旅遊的觀光客增加了
 (B) 西雅圖空著的公寓越來越少
 (C) 西雅圖公寓的興建很繁盛

內容　Seattle's apartment rental market gets tighter as computer enthusiasts move here, looking for jobs.

中譯　因為有許多電腦迷移入西雅圖找工作,使得該地的公寓出租市場漸漸供不應求。

解答　(B)

解說　apartment rental market 是「公寓出租市場」之意,指房屋、大樓等出租業務的一部分。Seattle's apartment rental market 的說法可替換為 the apartment rental market in Seattle。get tighter 為「變得緊縮」,意指要租公寓的人變多了,使得公寓的供給量越來越不足。「公寓」的英文是 apartment(英式英文用 flat),而各住戶分別持有產權的公寓大樓則稱作 condominium。enthusiast 為「狂熱者,(…的)迷」,computer enthusiast 則意指「電腦迷」。此外,move 為「搬家」,look for jobs 為「找工作」之意。

Listening Step 1

 請聽《Track 18》的會話後回答下面問題。

會話中的男士在找怎樣的房子？
- (A) 不在乎大小，但必須是靠近市中心的房子
- (B) 在市中心附近，有兩個房間的公寓
- (C) 租金便宜、靠近郊外的公寓

解答   (B)

Listening Step 2

熟悉下列關鍵字

complex   公寓社區
rent   *v.* 出租；*n.* 租金
availability   可得到的東西
incredible   難以置信的
refer   介紹，使求助
limited   有限的，為數不多的
prefer   寧願；偏好
open to   願意接受（～）的
desperate   絕望的
two-bedroom apartment   兩房公寓
one-bedroom apartment   單房公寓
home office   家庭辦公室，家庭工作室
loft   閣樓
acceptable   可接受的，可允許的
apartment manager   公寓管理員

② 請聽《Track 19》並在括弧內填入正確答案。

1. I'm sorry, but every apartment in this (   ) has been rented.
2. That's (   )!
3. Can you (   ) me anywhere else?
4. I'm kind of (   ) now.
5. Would a one-bedroom apartment with a loft be (   )?

解答

1. I'm sorry, but every apartment in this (complex) has been rented.
2. That's (incredible)!
3. Can you (refer) me anywhere else?
4. I'm kind of (desperate) now.
5. Would a one-bedroom apartment with a loft be (acceptable)?

② 請再聽一次《Track 18》的會話後回答下面問題。

1. 只有單一房間的公寓位於哪裡?
  (A) Edmonds
  (B) Redding
  (C) Redding 的附近

2. 有兩間房間的公寓租金要多少?
  (A) 1100 美元
  (B) 1350 美元
  (C) 1400 美元

解答   1. (A)   2. (C)

Listening Step 3

熟悉下列語句

② 請聽《Track 20》並在括弧內填入正確答案。

1. We have (　　) (　　　　) until December.
2. Are you open to an area (　　) (　　) out of town?
3. I'm (　　) (　　　) desperate now.
4. I can (　　) (　　) my home office in one bedroom.
5. Can I (　　) (　　) (　　) at the one-bedroom apartment with a loft now?

解答

1. We have (no) (availability) until December.
2. Are you open to an area (a) (bit) out of town?
3. I'm (kind) (of) desperate now.
4. I can (set) (up) my home office in one bedroom.
5. Can I (take) (a) (look) at the one-bedroom apartment with a loft now?

請再聽一次《Track 18》的會話後回答下面問題。

1. 會話中的男士為何感到沮喪?
   (A) 因為找不到工作
   (B) 因為找不到房子
   (C) 因為付不出房租

2. 會話中的男士為什麼覺得靠近市中心的房子比較好?
   (A) 因為比較便利
   (B) 因為不用花時間在開車上
   (C) 因為建築物較現代

3. 會話中的男士接下來要做什麼?
   (A) 訂定租賃契約
   (B) 找工作
   (C) 看看位於 Ashton 大道上的房子

解答　　　　　　　　　　　　　1. (B)　2. (B)　3. (C)

Speaking

會話

 請再聽一次《Track 18》。

Rental Agent: I'm sorry, but every apartment in this complex has been rented and we have no availability until December.

Daniel: That's incredible! Do you have any other apartment complex with availability? Can you refer me anywhere? I really need to find a place to stay.

Rental Agent: We do have several other complexes with limited availability. Do you prefer the downtown area or are you open to an area a bit out of town?

Daniel: Well, I would rather be closer to town for work, but I'm kind of desperate now. What do you have?

Rental Agent: Do you need a two-bedroom apartment or will a one-bedroom apartment do?

Daniel: I'd like a two-bedroom apartment if there is one available so that I can set up my home office in one bedroom.

Rental Agent: I see. So would a one-bedroom apartment with a loft be acceptable?

Daniel: Sure.

Rental Agent: Well, I have 2 one bedroom's, one with a loft, in Edmonds, and a two bedroom a little farther out near Redding.

Daniel: How much is the rent for each apartment?

Rental Agent: The one bedroom is $1,100, the one bedroom with a loft is $1,350 and the two bedroom is $1,400.

Daniel: That is not a big rent difference between the loft and two bedroom, but I would prefer not to have to drive so far. May I please get the address so I can take a look at the one-bedroom apartment with a loft now?

Rental Agent: Sure. The address is 4253 Ashton Drive. Sue Martin is the apartment manager there. I will let her know that you are coming.

出租經紀人：很抱歉，這一區所有的公寓都已經租出去了，在十
　　　　　　二月之前將不會有空房。

丹尼爾：這真是令人難以置信！妳還有沒有其他的公寓可以出租，
　　　　或是幫我介紹其他地方？我實在很需要找到地方落腳。

出租經紀人：我們的確還剩下一些其他的公寓可以出租。你喜歡
　　　　　　靠近市中心的公寓還是郊區也無所謂？

丹尼爾：為了工作上的方便，最好是能靠近市區一些，不過我現
　　　　在真的有點急了。妳有什麼樣的公寓呢？

出租經紀人：你要有兩個房間的公寓，還是單房的公寓即可？

丹尼爾：有兩個房間的公寓比較好，這樣我可以把其中一間佈置
　　　　成辦公室。

出租經紀人：我明白了。那麼，你可以接受只有一間房間再加一
　　　　　　個閣樓的公寓嗎？

丹尼爾：沒問題。

出租經紀人：那麼，我現在有兩間單房的公寓在愛德蒙，其中一
　　　　　　間有閣樓，還有一間兩房不過比較遠的公寓在雷丁。

丹尼爾：它們的房租各是多少？

出租經紀人：單房的房租是 1,100，單房加閣樓的是 1,350，兩房
　　　　　　的則是 1,400。

丹尼爾：有閣樓的和兩房的公寓房租似乎沒差多少，不過我寧願
　　　　選擇開車距離較近的。能不能請妳給我那間單房但有閣
　　　　樓的公寓地址？我現在就要過去看看。

出租經紀人：當然。公寓的地址是愛須頓大道 4253 號。那裡的公
　　　　　　寓管理員是蘇‧馬丁，我會通知她你要過去參觀。

語 法

- apartment 與 apartment building

  中文的「公寓」指的是整棟的建築物，但英文的 apartment 則通常指由一間一間的房間組成的一戶，建築物則以 apartment house 或 apartment building 稱之。complex 也可以說成 apartment complex，指的是由幾棟的 apartment building 所組成的大型公寓社區。「我住在公寓」的英文是 I live in an apartment.，「我的公寓位於山頂大道上」則是 My apartment building is on Hilltop Drive.。

- 不定詞的否定

  不定詞的否定形式，是必須將 not 直接置於不定詞之前。例如會話中的 I would prefer not to have to drive so far. 就不能說成 I would prefer to not have to drive so far.。

Speaking Function 11

詢問喜歡哪一個、說明喜歡哪一個

 請聽《Track 21》。

1. A: Do you prefer a one-bedroom apartment or a two-bedroom apartment?

   B: Oh, I think I'd like a two-bedroom apartment better.

2. A: Would you rather go there by yourself?

   B: No, I'd rather have someone come with me.

3. A: I prefer beer to wine.

   B: Oh, really? I don't like beer. I prefer wine.

解說

● 詢問兩者之間喜歡哪一個的說法中，除了 Do you like A or B? 之

外，也可以利用 prefer 這個字，說成 Do you prefer A or B?。語氣
若要更為恭敬，則說 Would you prefer A or B?。除了上述的說法
之外，還有 Do you prefer A to B?，這句話的意思是「你喜歡 A 勝
過 B 嗎?」。因此，若要詢問他人「比起咖啡來，你比較喜歡紅茶
嗎?」就可以說 Do you prefer tea to coffee?。另外，也可以使用疑
問詞 which，說成 Which do you prefer, tea or coffee?。

● Would you rather...? 也是詢問對方喜好的一種表達方式。Would
you rather go by yourself? 是「你寧可自己一個人去嗎?」的意思。
若用了 than，說成 Would you rather go by yourself than (go) with
someone? 則是「與其和他人同行，你寧可自己一個人去嗎?」。此
外，若使用「Would you rather + 人 + 動詞過去式」的形式，則為
「你希望某人做…嗎?」的意思，例如: Would you rather I paid now
or later? (你要我現在付費還是待會兒再付?)。

● 「比起 B 來，比較喜歡 A」的說法除了 I like A better than B. 或是
I prefer A to B. 之外，I'd rather go for A than B. / A seems better
than B. / A appeals to me more than B. 等說法也適用。例如 I like
wine better than beer. 可替換成 I prefer wine to beer. / I'd rather go
for wine than beer. / Wine seems better than beer. / Wine appeals to
me more than beer. 等句子。

練習 1【代換】

 請隨《Track 22》做代換練習。

1. Do you prefer *a condominium or a house?*

　　　　　　　　　　　　a downtown area or the suburbs?
　　　　　　　　　　　　jazz or classical music?
　　　　　　　　　　　　a small car or a medium car?
　　　　　　　　　　　　the red one or the blue one?

2. Would you rather *have a soft drink?*

> eat fast food?
>
> go by train?
>
> stay home tonight?
>
> rent an apartment?

3. *I prefer* a two-bedroom apartment *to* a one-bedroom apartment.

> I like ~ better than...
>
> I'd rather rent ~ than...
>
> I'd rather go for ~ than...
>
> ~ seems better than...
>
> ~ appeals to me more than...

練習 2【角色扮演】

 請隨《Track 23》在嗶一聲後唸出灰色部分的句子。

1. A: Do you prefer a hardcover or a paperback?

   B: Well, I think I'd like a paperback better.

2. A: Would you rather take private lessons?

   B: No, I'd rather join a class.

3. A: I prefer reading books to watching TV.

   B: Same here. Watching TV is just wasting time.

練習 3【覆誦重要語句】

 請隨《Track 24》覆誦英文句子。

1. availability 「可得到的東西」

↳ We must make sure every worker has the availability of a laptop computer.

（我們必須確認每一位員工都能擁有筆記型電腦。）

2. incredible 「難以置信的」

↳ It is incredible that he made the software and became a billionaire.

（真是無法相信他能設計出這套軟體並且成為百萬富翁。）

3. refer 「介紹，使求助」

↳ My doctor referred me to a heart specialist in New York.

（我的醫生幫我介紹了一位紐約的心臟專家。）

4. open to 「願意接受（～）的」

↳ Are you open to the nightshift?（你能接受值夜班嗎?）

5. kind of 「有一點」

↳ He's kind of jealous of my achievement.

（他對我的成就有一點忌妒。）

6. will do 「滿足需求，夠應付」

↳ Will 20 bottles of wine and 50 bottles of beer do for the reception?

（20 瓶葡萄酒加 50 瓶啤酒，足夠應付招待會嗎?）

7. set up 「建立，設立」

↳ Will you set up the computer on this desk while I attend a meeting?（在我去開會的這段時間，麻煩你把電腦安裝在這張桌子上好嗎?）

8. acceptable 「可接受的，可允許的」

↳ Sorry, but your business proposition is not acceptable.

（抱歉，我們無法接受你所提的企劃案。）

9. prefer not to 「寧願不要」

    ↳ I prefer not to speak about the matter at this moment.

    （我不想現在談論這件事。）

10. take a look 「看一眼」

    ↳ Will you please take a look at this figure?

    （請幫我看一下這個數字好嗎?）

實力測驗

你正在跟另一半商量買新車的事情。你的另一半說買家庭房車 (sedan)
就好，但你卻傾向於購買休旅車（SUV〈sport-utility vehicle〉或 RV
〈recreational vehicle〉），請試著以三種不同的說法向另一半表達你比
較喜歡休旅車的想法。

參考解答

1. I prefer an SUV to a sedan.

2. I'd rather buy an SUV than a sedan.

3. An SUV appeals to me more than a sedan.

Advertising 廣 告

Listening

Warm-up / Pre-questions

 請聽《Track 25》的新聞快報後回答下面問題。

Treckers Collection Footwear 將在下個月初進行什麼活動?
(A) 推出秋季的新商品
(B) 在全國各地舉辦拍賣會
(C) 與別家公司合併

內容 Treckers Collection Footwear is expected to unleash its new line of footwear for the fall early next month. The company's footwear, designed for comfort, longevity, and style, has been the rave of fashion magazines since last year.

中譯 崔克皮鞋預計將在下個月初推出他們的秋季新款鞋。這間公司的鞋款是以舒適、耐穿、引領時尚為設計宗旨,自去年起便為許多流行雜誌所一致推崇。

解答 (A)

解說 Treckers Collection Footwear 是皮鞋公司的名稱。footwear 是「鞋類」的總稱,為不可數名詞。footwear 包含了 shoes, boots, sandals 等,運動鞋則稱作 sneakers。unleash 雖為「解放」之意,但在這裡則用作「發表」。line 除了「線」之外,也有「商品」之意。comfort 為「舒適」、longevity 為「長壽」、rave 為「極力推薦,激賞」之意。

Listening Step 1

 請聽《Track 26》的會話後回答下面問題。

兩個人在談論什麼話題？
(A) 關於廣告費用
(B) 關於廣告業者的選定
(C) 關於廣告活動

解答　　　　　　　　　　　　　　　　　　　　(C)

Listening Step 2

熟悉下列關鍵字

advertising campaign　一系列的廣告活動
effective　有效的
launching-pad year　新品上市的第一年
consumer　消費者
range　範圍
youngster　年輕人
professional　專業人士，專家
once　一旦
fashionable　時髦
advertisement　廣告
run　上（廣告）
major　主要的
metropolitan　大都會的
overseas　海外的
shortly　馬上，很短的時間之後
primary　主要的

focus　中心，焦點
market　市場
package　完整一套（例如廣告案）
region　地區

② 請聽《Track 27》並在括弧內填入正確答案。

1. Do you think the new advertising campaign will be as
   (　　　　) as last year's?
2. The (　　　　) loved us.
3. The advertisements will be running in every (　　　) fashion
   magazine.
4. Our (　　　　) campaign will follow shortly after in
   September.
5. Our primary marketing (　　　) will be Europe.

解答
1. Do you think the new advertising campaign will be as (effective) as last
   year's?
2. The (consumers) loved us.
3. The advertisements will be running in every (major) fashion magazine.
4. Our (overseas) campaign will follow shortly after in September.
5. Our primary marketing (focus) will be Europe.

② 請再聽一次《Track 26》的會話後回答下面問題。

1. Treckers Collection Footwear 的消費群在哪一個年齡層?
   (A) 十多歲的年輕世代
   (B) 中年的上班族

(C) 從年輕人到中年人都有

2. 美國國內的廣告活動將從何時開始？

(A) 8 月

(B) 9 月

(C) 10 月

解答	1. (C)　2. (A)

Listening Step 3

熟悉下列語句

as effective as　和～一樣有效
What is not to like?　還有什麼可以挑剔的？（強調非常滿意）
in between　在中間
try on　試穿
sell oneself　自我銷售
shortly after　在～之後立刻
Let's see if...　讓我們來看看是否…

②請聽《Track 28》並在括弧內填入正確答案。

1. Do you think the new advertising campaign will be (　　　)
(　　　) (　　　) last year's?

2. What is (　　　) (　　　) (　　　) ?

3. Once you have (　　　) a pair (　　　), the shoes sell themselves.

4. Our overseas campaign will follow (　　　) (　　　) in September.

5. Let's (   ) (   ) we can make that happen in our Asian markets as well.

解答

1. Do you think the new advertising campaign will be (as) (effective) (as) last year's?
2. What is (not) (to) (like) ?
3. Once you have (tried) a pair (on), the shoes sell themselves.
4. Our overseas campaign will follow (shortly) (after) in September.
5. Let's (see) (if) we can make that happen in our Asian markets as well.

② 請再聽一次《Track 26》的會話後回答下面問題。

1. 行銷總監認為新的廣告活動如何?
   (A) 與去年相同，或比去年效果好
   (B) 與去年相同，或比去年效果差
   (C) 將會帶來歷年最好的效果

2. 廣告利用了什麼媒體做宣傳?
   (A) 流行雜誌與電視
   (B) 流行雜誌與報紙
   (C) 流行雜誌與車廂廣告

3. 海外的行銷重點為何放在歐洲?
   (A) 因為顧客最多
   (B) 因為競爭最激烈
   (C) 因為可以塑造出高級品的印象

解答   1. (A)   2. (B)   3. (A)

Speaking

會話

 請再聽一次《Track 26》。

Marketing Agent: Do you think the new advertising campaign will be as effective as last year's?

Marketing Director: Oh, absolutely. Last year was our launching-pad year. The consumers loved us. This year will be even better.

Marketing Agent: I'm glad you are pleased with the campaign.

Marketing Director: What is not to like? We have made our shoes appealing to a wide range of people from youngsters to older professionals and everyone in between.

Marketing Agent: Once you have tried a pair on, the shoes sell themselves. They are so comfortable.

Marketing Director: And fashionable.

Marketing Agent: The advertisements will be running in every major fashion magazine and Sunday newspaper in every major metropolitan area starting in August.

Marketing Director: That's very good. Our overseas campaign will follow shortly after in September.

Marketing Agent: That's correct. Our primary marketing focus will be Europe since they were our largest group of consumers outside the U. S. last year.

Marketing Director: Let's see if we can make that happen in our

Asian markets as well. Can you pull out the advertising package for that region and let's have a look at it?

中　譯 ··

行銷經紀：你認為我們新推出的一系列廣告會如去年一樣成功嗎？

行銷總監：嗯，絕對沒問題。去年我們才剛上市便大受顧客喜愛，今年一定會更成功。

行銷經紀：我很高興你能對這個系列廣告滿意。

行銷總監：還有什麼可以挑剔的？我們的鞋子吸引了廣大的顧客，從一般年輕人到較高齡的專業人士，涵蓋其中每一個年齡層的消費者，大家都喜歡。

行銷經紀：任何人只要親身試穿我們的鞋子後，不用任何多餘的推銷，就能吸引其購買。因為它們穿起來實在是非常舒適。

行銷總監：而且樣式時髦！

行銷經紀：從八月開始，我們將會在各大都會區的每一份大型時尚雜誌與週日報上面刊登廣告。

行銷總監：很好！我們的海外系列廣告則會在九月初接著登場。

行銷經紀：沒錯！去年歐洲是我們在美國以外的最大消費市場，因此我們將會鎖定歐洲為我們的重點市場。

行銷總監：讓我們等著看在亞洲市場能不能也這麼成功。請你把亞洲區的廣告案拿出來，讓我們來研究一下。

語　法 ··

● 強調比較級時的 even

通常 even 為表「甚至」之意的副詞，但用於強調比較級時，則為「還

要」、「更加」。其用法如：Your golf club is very good, but mine is *even better*. (你的高爾夫球桿很不錯，但是我的更好)。

● 「在中間」之意的 in between

in between 可用於表時間上或空間上的「在中間」之意。其用法如：I have two meetings this afternoon and I'll talk to you *in between*. (今天下午我有兩個會議，我將在會議空檔與你談談。) / It's somewhere *in between* Los Angeles and San Diego. (它位於洛杉磯與聖地牙哥之間的某個地方。)

● 多語意的 run

run 除了「跑」之外，還有很多不同的語意，茲舉數個主要用法如下：

「經營」: She *runs* a restaurant in town. (她在城裡開了家餐廳。)

「(機械等) 運轉」: The engine *is running*. (引擎在運轉。)

「流出」: The tap *is running*. (水龍頭的水在流。)

「上映」: The movie *runs* for two hours. (這部電影的播映時間為兩個小時。)

「競選」: He *is running* for President. (他參與競選總統。)

「有效」: The contract *runs* for three years. (契約三年內有效。)

「刊載」: The advertisement *runs* in the newspaper. (廣告刊登在報紙上。)

Speaking Function 12

「贊同」「不贊同」的說法

 請聽《Track 29》。

1. A: Do you think this plan is all right?

   B: Yes, that's very good.

2. A: Can I have your opinion on this business plan?

B: I entirely approve of that.

3. A: I think we should break off business relations with them.

   B: I don't approve of that.

解說

● 詢問對方是否贊同某件事情時，最基本的詢問方式便是 Do you think ~ is/are all right?。例如：「你覺得這個計畫可行嗎?」說成 Do you think this plan is all right?，「這份報告可以嗎?」則是 Do you think this report is all right?。此外，也可以用表示「認同」的 approve、表示「贊成」的 in favor of、表示「可接受」的 acceptable，說成 Do you approve of this plan? / Are you in favor of this plan? / Is this plan acceptable?，而 Does this plan meet with your approval? 則是略為正式的詢問方式。

● 贊同的情況下，可以採取 Yes, that's very good.（那非常好）這樣直接回答好壞的方式，或是採取如 I approve of that.（我贊同），以表示「贊同」之意的方式直接回答。屬於前者的回答方式還有 I'm very happy about that. / That's just what I wanted. / That's just what I had in mind.（我也這麼想）/ That sounds just fine. 等。屬於後者則有 I think I can give that my full approval. / I find that quite acceptable. / I can see no reason to oppose that.（我找不到反對的理由）/ I would like to endorse that.（我支持）等的回答方式。

● 不贊同的情況下，則可以用 approve 的否定，說成 I don't approve of that.；也可以用 approve 的反義字 disapprove，說成 I disapprove of that.。此外，還有下列說法：I cannot give my approval to that. / I'm not in favor of that. / I'm not very happy about that.。

練習 1【代換】

②請隨《Track 30》做代換練習。

1. *Do you think* this report *is all right?*

   Do you approve of...?
   Are you in favor of...?
   Is... acceptable?
   Does... meet with your approval?

2. "Do you think this program is all right?"
   "*Yes, that's very good.*"

   "Yes, I'm very happy about that."
   "Yes, that's just what I wanted."
   "Yes, that's just what I had in mind."
   "Yes, that sounds just fine."

3. *I entirely approve of* that.

   I think we can give... our full approval.
   I find... quite acceptable.
   I can see no reason to oppose...
   I would like to endorse...

4. *I don't approve of*   that.

   I disapprove of
   I cannot give my approval to
   I'm not in favor of
   I'm not very happy about

練習 2【角色扮演】

 請隨《Track 31》在嗶一聲後唸出灰色部分的句子。

   1. A: Do you think this outline is all right?

B: Yes, that's very good.

2. A: Can I have your opinion on this budget proposal?

B: I entirely approve of that.

3. A: The only solution is to stop the production line.

B: I don't approve of that.

練習 3【覆誦重要語句】

 請隨《Track 32》覆誦英文句子。

1. as A as B 「和 B 一樣 A」
   ↳ Do you think the new secretary is as efficient as Nancy?
   （你認為新來的秘書會和南西一樣能幹嗎?）

2. even better 「更好」
   ↳ This is even better than her debut album.
   （她這次的專輯比第一張更棒。）

3. appealing 「有吸引力的」
   ↳ I find the position offered by the company very appealing. （我覺得這家公司所提供的職位非常誘人。）

4. a wide range of 「廣泛的」
   ↳ This store deals with a wide range of kitchen utensils.
   （這家商店販賣各式各樣的廚房用品。）

5. in between 「在中間」
   ↳ There are two big buildings and a small shrine in between. （在兩棟大建築物之間有一座小廟。）

6. once 「一旦」
   ↳ Once you hear her voice, you'll never forget it.
   （你一旦聽過她的聲音，便永遠不會忘懷。）

7. try on　「試穿」

　↳I wonder if I could try on this sweater.

　（不知道可不可以試穿這件毛衣?）

8. run　「登載」

　↳We decided not to run the advertisement in the newspaper.（我們決定不在報紙上刊登廣告。）

9. shortly after　「在～之後立刻」

　↳One of the plane's engines caught fire shortly after takeoff.

　（飛機起飛之後不久，其中一具引擎便起火燃燒。）

10. Let's see if...　「讓我們來看看是否…」

　↳Let's see if we have ordered all that we need for the convention.（讓我們來看看是不是已經將會議所需的物品都訂購好了。）

實力測驗

你的下屬提議公司旅遊 (company trip) 可以去夏威夷。請試著以三種不同的說法表示你的贊同。

參考解答	1. That's a very good idea. 2. I find the idea quite acceptable. 3. I approve of the idea.

Fitness 健 身

Listening

Warn-up / Pre-questions

 請聽《Track 33》的商業廣告後回答下面問題。

這則廣告有哪一點吸引人?
  (A) 最新的設備
  (B) 堅強的指導陣容
  (C) 優惠的價格折扣

內容　Spring is almost here! Let Model Fitness Center help you lose those winter pounds and tighten up those muscles with our 20 percent discount special.

中譯　春天即將來臨! 模特兒健身中心現正推出八折特惠專案,幫助您減去冬天累積的贅肉,並讓您的肌肉更加結實!

解答　(C)

解說　使用於「幫助人做~」之意的 help,在口語中通常與原形動詞連用。即原為 Will you help me to clear the table? 的句子,在口語中會省略 to,說成 Will you help me clear the table?。其他: lose 為「失去」、winter pounds 為「冬天增加的體重」、tighten up 為「使變緊」、muscle 為「肌肉」之意。複數的 muscles 指的則是身體各個部位的肌肉。

Listening Step 1

 請聽《Track 34》的會話後回答下面問題。

對話中的兩個人在擔心什麼?

(A) 變得太胖了

(B) 運動不足

(C) 工作上的壓力

解答   (A)

Listening Step 2

熟悉下列關鍵字

over   在～期間

fasten   繫上;扣住

stuck   被困住(stick 的過去式及過去分詞)

discount   減價

gym   健身房(gymnasium 的縮略)

encourage   鼓勵,打氣

drag   拖曳

hate   討厭,憎惡

aerobics   有氧運動

cardiovascular training   強化心機能的訓練

weight lifting   舉重

muscle building   強化肌肉

league   聯盟

lunch hour   午餐時間;午休時間

routine   每日固定的行程;例行公事

② 請聽《Track 35》並在括弧內填入正確答案。

1. My pants don't (　　　　) very well anymore.
2. If we both go to the gym, we can (　　　　) each other.
3. That way I can (　　　　) you away from your desk and make you go.
4. I (　　　　) going to the gym alone.
5. They have (　　　　) classes for cardiovascular training.

解答

1. My pants don't (fasten) very well anymore.
2. If we both go to the gym, we can (encourage) each other.
3. That way I can (drag) you away from your desk and make you go.
4. I (hate) going to the gym alone.
5. They have (aerobics) classes for cardiovascular training.

② 請再聽一次《Track 34》的會話後回答下面問題。

1. 對話中的兩個人決定做什麼？
   (A) 節食
   (B) 上健身房
   (C) 接受每週兩次的有氧課程

2. 兩個人何時要去報名？
   (A) 講完話之後馬上去
   (B) 中午休息時間
   (C) 下班之後

解答　　　　　　　　　　　　1. (B)　　2. (B)

Listening Step 3

熟悉下列語句

> put on a few too many pounds　增加了不少磅（的體重）
> go on a diet　開始節食
> it's really starting to show　結果開始顯現
> So do I.　我也是。
> That'd be great.　太棒了。

②　請聽《Track 36》並在括弧內填入正確答案。

1. I've (　　) (　　) a few too many pounds over the holidays.

2. I need to go (　　) (　　) (　　).

3. It's really (　　) (　　) (　　).

4. (　　) (　　) (　　).

5. (　　) (　　) (　　).

解答

1. I've (put) (on) a few too many pounds over the holidays.

2. I need to go (on) (a) (diet).

3. It's really (starting) (to) (show).

4. (So) (do) (I).

5. (That'd) (be) (great).

②　請再聽一次《Track 34》的會話後回答下面問題。

1. Scott 為何發胖？

(A) 休假期間幾乎沒外出

    (B) 吃了太多富含脂肪的食物

    (C) 最近這陣子只顧工作，運動量不足

2. Scott 和其友人都討厭什麼？

    (A) 與女生一起做有氧運動

    (B) 自己一個人去健身房

    (C) 節食

3. Scott 和其友人要上健身房做什麼？

    (A) 做有氧運動與舉重訓練

    (B) 做有氧運動與打籃球

    (C) 做舉重訓練與打籃球

解答   1. (C)   2. (B)   3. (C)

═══ Speaking ═══

會話

 請再聽一次《Track 34》。

Tom: I think I've put on a few too many pounds over the holidays, Scott. I need to go on a diet. My pants don't fasten very well anymore.

Scott: I know exactly what you mean. I've been stuck behind my desk for 12 hours a day for the last two months and it's really starting to show.

Tom: I saw an advertisement for a discount at Model Fitness Center. Would you be interested in signing up?

Scott: That's a good idea. If we both go to the gym, we can encourage each other.

Tom: That way I can drag you away from your desk and make you go. Besides, I hate going to the gym alone.

Scott: So do I. What kind of programs do they have there?

Tom: Well, they have aerobics classes for cardiovascular training and weight lifting classes for muscle building.

Scott: I'm not really interested in aerobics. I would rather play a sport for my cardiovascular exercise.

Tom: They also have men's basketball leagues that run every 6 weeks.

Scott: That'd be great. Maybe we'll do a little weight lifting and then play basketball twice a week.

Tom: So, shall we go and sign up during our lunch hour today?

Scott: Sure. The sooner we get started on a new fitness routine, the better.

中　譯 ....

湯　　姆： 史考特，放假期間我好像又胖了幾磅，我得開始節食了。我的褲子簡直就要扣不上了。

史考特： 我非常能夠體會你的感受。過去兩個月來，我平均每天被困在座位上長達十二個小時，現在「成果」也慢慢浮現了。

湯　　姆： 我在廣告上看到模特兒健身中心正在舉辦特價優惠。你有沒有興趣報名？

史考特： 這真是個好主意。假如我們能一起上健身房，我們就可

以彼此鼓勵。

湯　姆：這樣一來我就可以把你從座位上拖走，強迫你去健身。
　　　　再說，我也很討厭自己一個人上健身房。

史考特：我也是。他們提供了哪些健身課程呢？

湯　姆：喔，他們有強化心機能的有氧課程與強化肌肉的舉重課
　　　　程。

史考特：我對有氧課程實在不感興趣。我比較喜歡以運動競賽的
　　　　方式來鍛鍊心臟機能。

湯　姆：他們也有男子籃球聯盟，每六週為一期。

史考特：那太棒了。我們也許可以做些舉重訓練再加上每週打兩
　　　　次籃球。

湯　姆：那麼我們何不利用今天的午休時間去報名？

史考特：好啊，我們能愈早開始定期健身愈好。

語　法

● 表示期間的 over

over 除了可以表示空間上「跨越～」外，也可以表示時間上「在～期間一直」的意思。其用法如 I've put on a few too many pounds *over* the holidays. 表示「我在假期中胖了不少」。其他例句如：I went to see my mother in New York *over* the weekend.（我利用週末去紐約探望母親）/ He produced 20 albums *over* a period of three years.（他在三年間製作了 20 張專輯）/ Let's talk about it *over* lunch.（讓我們邊吃邊談吧）。

● both 的用法

both 有形容詞、代名詞、副詞等三種詞性，因為形容詞是用來修飾名詞，所以用法如 You're burning the candle at *both* ends.（你太過勉強自己了）。而代名詞的用法為 I know *both* of them.（他們兩個我都認識），或是置於主詞或受詞的後面當作同位語，如 We *both* went to the gym.

（我們都上健身房）。副詞的用法則為 both A and B（AB 兩者都）的
型態，例如：She can speak *both* English and Spanish.（她會說英文也
會說西班牙文）。

● So do I. 與 So am I. 的差別
So do I. 與 So am I. 都譯成「我也是」，但是 So do I. 用於對應主要子
句的動詞為 like 或 study 等一般動詞的情形，而 So am I. 則用於對應
be 動詞的情形。其用法如：I like jazz. — *So do I.* / I'm interested in jazz.
— *So am I.*。

Speaking Function 13

詢問是否感興趣、回答有無興趣

 請聽《Track 37》。

1. A: Are you interested in scuba diving?
   B: Yes, it's one of my favorite watersports.
2. A: What are your interests?
   B: I'm interested in pottery.
3. A: They are having a modern art exhibition at the city museum.
   B: Well, I'm not very interested in modern art.

解說
● 詢問對方對某件事情是否感興趣時，最基本的詢問方式便是 Are
you interested in ～?，將感興趣的事物置於介系詞 in 的後面。例
如想詢問對方是否對潛水感興趣時，便可說 Are you interested in
scuba diving?。此外，也可以將感興趣的事物當作主詞，說成 Does
scuba diving interest you? 或 Does scuba diving appeal to you?；或者
是將感興趣的事物當作受詞，以 Do you find scuba diving

interesting? 的方式詢問。其他也可以用 Do you have any interest in scuba diving? 或 Do you go for scuba diving? 的方式詢問。若要問他人「你的興趣是什麼?」則可用 What are you interested in? 或 What are your interests?。

客氣地邀約他人「你有沒有興趣做〜」的說法,則是 Would you be interested in 〜?,例如: Would you be interested in going to the reggae concert? (你有沒有興趣聽雷鬼演唱會?) / Would you be interested in taking piano lessons? (你想不想去上鋼琴課?)。

● 說明個人興趣的基本說法是 I'm interested in 〜.。例如對陶器有興趣,便可說 I'm interested in pottery.;或是用名詞 interest,說成 I have a great interest in pottery. 或 My particular interest is pottery.。此外,Pottery interests me a great deal. / I find pottery very interesting. / I go for pottery in a big way. (我非常喜歡陶器) 等說法也行。

● 對某件事不感興趣時,可以用否定句的形式傳達。例如「我對現代美術沒什麼興趣」為 I'm not very interested in modern art.,或是 I don't find modern art interesting. / I find modern art rather uninteresting. / I don't have much interest in modern art.。此外,還可以一併記住 Modern art isn't for me. 及 Modern art leaves me cold. 的用法。

練習 1【代換】

 請隨《Track 38》做代換練習。

1. *Are you interested in* gardening?

Does... interest you?

Do you find... interesting?

Do you go for...?

Does... appeal to you?
Do you have any interest in...?

2. Would you be interested in *going to the reggae concert?*
   joining our club?
   signing up for the summer trip?
   taking a sunset cruise?
   conducting a survey?

3. *I'm interested in* pottery.
   I have a great interest in...
   My particular interest is...
   ... interests me a great deal.
   I find... very interesting.
   I go for... in a big way.

4. *I'm not very interested in* classical music.
   I don't find... very interesting.
   I find... rather uninteresting.
   I don't have much interest in...
   ... isn't for me.
   ... leaves me cold.

練習 2【角色扮演】

 請隨《Track 39》在嗶一聲後唸出灰色部分的句子。

1. A: Are you interested in tennis?

   B: Yes, it's one of my favorite sports.

2. A: What are your interests?

   B: I'm interested in quilting.

3. A: They are having a Picasso exhibition at the Tate Gallery.

   B: Well, I'm not very interested in abstract paintings.

練習 3【覆誦重要語句】

 請隨《Track 40》覆誦英文句子。

1. put on　「增加」

   ↳ You seem to have put on weight over the winter holidays.

   （你似乎在寒假期間變胖了一些。）

2. go on a diet　「開始節食」

   ↳ My doctor told me I should go on a diet.

   （我的醫生告訴我最好要開始節食。）

3. fasten　「繫上；扣住」

   ↳ Will you please fasten the seatbelt?

   （請把安全帶繫上好嗎?）

4. exactly　「精確地；完全地」

   ↳ I know exactly how you feel now.

   （我完全明白你現在的感受。）

5. stick　「使困住」

   ↳ He's been stuck in front of the computer all day today.

   （他今天一整天都不得不待在電腦前面。）

6. Would you be interested in...　「你有沒有興趣…」

   ↳ Would you be interested in signing up for the audition?

   （你有沒有興趣參加試鏡?）

7. both 「兩者都，兩人都」

  ↳We both take aerobics lessons twice a week at the gym.

  （我們倆一星期都在健身房上兩次的有氧課程。）

8. each other 「彼此」

  ↳Jack and Jim are good friends and they respect each other.（傑克和吉姆是彼此互相敬愛的好朋友。）

9. drag 「拖曳」

  ↳I can't drag Tom away from the cartoons on TV.

  （我實在沒辦法把湯姆從播放卡通的電視機前拉走。）

10. hate 「討厭，憎惡」

  ↳I hate hearing complaints from my colleagues.

  （我很討厭聽我同事發牢騷。）

實力測驗

你和朋友一起去紐約旅行，兩人正在商量明天的行程。你想前往參觀以收藏當代藝術 (contemporary art) 作品而聞名的古根漢美術館 (Guggenheim Museum)。請試著以三種不同的說法向朋友詢問他是否對當代藝術有興趣。

參考解答
1. Are you interested in contemporary art?
2. Do you have any interest in contemporary art?
3. Does contemporary art interest you?

Wage Increase 加 薪

Listening

Warm-up / Pre-questions

 請聽《Track 41》的新聞快報後回答下面問題。

哪些人的薪水將調漲,是自何時開始,並調漲多少個百分比?
 (A) 製造業勞工的薪水將自四月開始調漲 5%
 (B) 建築工人的薪水將自五月開始調漲 3%
 (C) 公務人員的薪水將自六月開始調漲 4%

內容 Construction workers throughout the state will receive a 3% pay increase starting in May as a result of a yearlong effort by the State Construction Workers Union.

中譯 由於過去一年來州建築工人工會的努力爭取,五月起全州的建築工人都將可以獲得百分之三的調薪。

解答 (B)

解說 pay 是口語中用以表示「薪水」之意的一般用語,而 wages 指的是支付給靠勞力工作者或工業技術人員的薪水,salary 指的則是辦公室的事務人員或是專業技術人員所領取的薪水。construction workers 為「建築工人」、throughout 為「遍布(某個地方)」、state 為「州」、pay increase 為「加薪」、as a result of 為「作為~的結果」、effort 為「努力」、union 為「工會」之意。

Listening Step 1

對話中的其中一位男士因何事而驚喜?

　　(A) 可以獲得臨時津貼

　　(B) 可以獲得加薪

　　(C) 可以獲得意外的獎金

解答　　　　　　　　　　　　　　　　　　　　　　　　　　(B)

Listening Step 2

熟悉下列關鍵字

hectic　忙碌的；緊張的

cost　花費

payday　發薪日

paycheck　付薪水的支票

pay raise　加薪

prove　證明

My goodness!　我的老天!

surprise　驚喜；驚訝

annual percentage increase　每年依百分比調增

base on　基於（base 通常用被動語態）

inflation　通貨膨脹

② 請聽《Track 43》並在括弧內填入正確答案。

　　1. It has been a really (　　　) week.

　　2. I'm so glad it's (　　　).

　　3. Have you picked up your (　　　) yet?

4. The pay (   ) just kicked in and every bit helps.

5. My goodness! This is some (   )!

解答

1. It has been a really (hectic) week.

2. I'm so glad it's (payday).

3. Have you picked up your (paycheck) yet?

4. The pay (raise) just kicked in and every bit helps.

5. My goodness! This is some (surprise)!

② 請再聽一次《Track 42》的會話後回答下面問題。

1. 今天是什麼日子?

(A) 發薪日

(B) 要求加薪的示威遊行日

(C) 特地加班的日子

2. 他們兩個人接下來要去哪裡?

(A) 工地

(B) 交涉加薪的地點

(C) 會計部門

解答   1. (A)   2. (C)

Listening Step 3

熟悉下列語句

set ～ back   使～延誤，妨礙

catch up   追趕

on schedule   依照進度

make it　成功; 做到

pick up　取; 拿

on one's way　在途中

Wait until you see your check.　我等著看你領到（薪水）支票的樣子。

kick in　開始生效

every bit helps　多少有點幫助

This is some surprise!　這真是一個驚喜!

get ～ through　使～通過; 完成

get over to　去到

② 請聽《Track 44》並在括弧內填入正確答案。

　　1. That rain last week really (　　) (　　) (　　).
　　2. Do you think we'll be (　　) (　　) by next week?
　　3. Have you (　　) (　　) your paycheck yet?
　　4. Well, the pay raise just (　　) (　　) and (　　)
　　　 (　　) helps.
　　5. I didn't think they would ever (　　) (　　) (　　)!

解答
1. That rain last week really (set) (us) (back).
2. Do you think we'll be (on) (schedule) by next week?
3. Have you (picked) (up) your paycheck yet?
4. Well, the pay raise just (kicked) (in) and (every) (bit) helps.
5. I didn't think they would ever (get) (that) (through)!

② 請再聽一次《Track 42》的會話後回答下面問題。

1. 為何工作的進度落後了?

(A) 因為下雨

(B) 因為工地發生了一些意外

(C) 因為要求加薪的抗爭活動

2. 預測下週會是什麼情況?

(A) 繼續罷工

(B) 下大雨

(C) 要加班

3. 對話中的其中一位男士對何事不表樂觀?

(A) 工作的進度

(B) 勞資雙方的談判

(C) 依據通貨膨脹率的每年調薪

解答　　　　　　　　　　　　　　1. (A)　2. (C)　3. (C)

Speaking

會話

 請再聽一次《Track 42》。

Bob: I'm so glad it's Friday. It has been a really hectic week.

Harry: I know. That rain last week really set us back and we've been trying to catch up all week.

Bob: Do you think we'll be on schedule by next week?

Harry: I think so. It may take us until Wednesday and cost us a few hours of overtime, but I think we'll make it. I'm so glad it's payday. I'm ready for the weekend.

Bob: Have you picked up your paycheck yet?

Harry: No. I'm on my way over to the office now. Do you want to walk over with me?

Bob: Sure. Wait until you see your check.

Harry: Why? What are you talking about?

Bob: Well, the pay raise just kicked in and every bit helps. I'm pretty excited about mine.

Harry: No! I don't believe it! We finally got the pay raise?

Bob: Yes, you can believe it. Here is my check to prove it. Look at this!

Harry: My goodness! This is some surprise! I didn't think they would ever get that through!

Bob: Not only that, they are trying to get us an annual percentage increase next year based on inflation.

Harry: Well, I'll believe that one when I see it! Let's get over to the office now so I can see what this increase looks like.

中　譯 ....

鮑伯：真高興今天是星期五，這個禮拜以來實在是夠忙碌的了。

哈利：是啊，上個禮拜下的那場雨延誤了進度，害得我們整個星期都在趕工。

鮑伯：你認為我們到下個禮拜能不能趕上進度?

哈利：應該可以。我們可能得要加班，並且至少要到星期三以後才有可能趕上進度，不過我想我們應該辦得到。真高興今天就是發薪水的日子，我已經準備好要去度週末了。

鮑伯：你領薪水了嗎?

哈利：還沒，我現在正要去辦公室，你要不要和我一起走過去？

鮑伯：好啊。我要等著看你領到薪水的樣子。

哈利：為什麼？什麼意思？

鮑伯：加薪條款正式生效了，薪水或多或少都會有點增加。我對於自己的薪資可是非常興奮呢。

哈利：喔！我不敢相信這是真的！我們終於加薪了嗎？

鮑伯：是的，你絕對可以相信，看看我的支票吧，這就是實證！

哈利：老天！這真是一個驚喜！我從沒想過他們會成功！

鮑伯：不僅如此，工會還在努力讓我們的薪資從明年起可以依據每年的通貨膨脹率等比增加。

哈利：嗯，這點就得眼見為憑了。我們現在就趕緊到辦公室去，看到底加了多少薪水。

語　法

● 關於 TGIF

會話中一開頭出現的 I'm so glad it's Friday. 這句話，與另外一種稱作 TGIF 的說法相似。TGIF 為 Thank God it's Friday. 的縮略，用以形容忙了一整個禮拜終於要迎接週末的喜悅。

● 關於 make it

make it 主要語意有四個：「順利完成」、「趕上（交通工具或約定的時間）」、「撿回性命」及「成功」，其用法如："Do you think we can finish this by Wednesday?" "Yes, I think we can *make it*."（「你認為我們可以在星期三之前完成嗎？」「我想應該可以」）/ "The train leaves in 10 minutes." "If we run, we should *make it*."（「火車將在 10 分鐘之後離站」「如果我們用跑的，應該能趕上」）/ Jack was in serious condition, but he *made it*.（傑克本來性命垂危，但他最後還是撿回一條命）/ I never thought Julie would *make it* as a singer.（我從沒想過茱麗能成功當上歌手）。

- yet 與 already 的差別

  在疑問句中，要表示「已經」的意思時，一般應該用 yet，若是用 already，則帶有驚訝或疑惑的語氣。例如若將 Have you written the letter *yet*?（你已經寫信了嗎?）句中的 yet 換成 already 的話：Have you written the letter *already*?（你已經寫信了啊?），就代表對此一事實感到吃驚或疑惑之意。

- 副詞 over 的語意

  副詞的 over 有「(越過～) 往另一邊的方向」或是「往這一邊的方向」兩種完全相反的語意。Let's walk *over* to the office.（讓我們走到辦公室）句中 over 的語意就是「往另外一邊的方向」。但下例 Why don't you come *over*?（你何不過來?）中的 over 就是「往這一邊的方向」的意思。

Speaking Function 14

表示驚訝的說法

 請聽《Track 45》。

1. A: Did you know this has sold 10 million copies all over the world?

   B: That's very surprising!

2. A: The board fired the president.

   B: What a surprise!

3. A: Joe was promoted to senior manager.

   B: I find it very surprising.

解說

● 英語中表示驚喜時可以用 wow 這個字，但也不能一路 Wow! 到

底，應該學學其他的表達方式。表示驚訝的語句通常採用「That's + 形容詞 + !」的基本型態，例如在 That's 之後接續 surprising, amazing, extraordinary, astonishing 等表示訝異的形容詞。當然，也可以用 That's a surprise! 此種接續名詞的形式，或是將 that 換成 this，說成 This is a surprise!。此外，some 在口語中有「了不起的、驚人的」之意，因此也可使用 This is some surprise! 強調驚訝的說法。

● 與 Wow! 類似，用來表示驚訝的說法還有 What a surprising! / How very surprising! / Good heavens! / My goodness! 等，而最後的兩個說法非常口語，為 native speaker 經常使用，學起來大為受用。此外，No! I don't believe it! 或 You don't say! 等也可使用於同樣的情況。

● 利用「I find it + 形容詞」的句型表達，即在形容詞之處換上 very surprising, astonishing, extraordinary, amazing, incredible 等詞語，也可以用來表示驚訝。這是對於對方所說之事表示「我對此深感訝異」的意思，可說是一種以冷靜態度表達驚訝的語句。

練習 1【代換】

② 請隨《Track 46》做代換練習。

1. That's *very surprising.*

> amazing!
> extraordinary!
> astonishing!
> a surprise!

2. "The president is here to see you."

   "*What a surprise!*"

   "How very surprising!"

"Good heavens!"
"My goodness!"
"No! I don't believe it!"
"You don't say!"

3. I find it *very surprising.*

astonishing.
extraordinary.
amazing.
incredible.

練習 2【角色扮演】

 請隨《Track 47》在嗶一聲後唸出灰色部分的句子。

1. A: That small condominium costs $600,000.

   B: That's very surprising!

2. A: We've got a special bonus.

   B: What a surprise!

3. A: I'm afraid your proposal was not accepted.

   B: I find it very surprising.

練習 3【覆誦重要語句】

 請隨《Track 48》覆誦英文句子。

1. hectic 「忙碌的；緊張的」

   ↳Because of my hectic schedule, I don't have much time for cooking.

   （由於我的時間表排得很緊，所以沒有時間做菜。）

2. set ～ back 「使～延誤；妨礙」

↳ The power failure set us back by a few hours.

（停電耽誤了我們數小時之久。）

3. catch up 「追上」

↳ I'll park the car and catch up.

（我把車停好後再趕上你們。）

4. on schedule 「依照時間表」

↳ His plane will arrive on schedule.

（他的班機將會準時抵達。）

5. make it 「成功；做到」

↳ The project wasn't very difficult so I could make it without any help.

（這項計畫並不算太困難，所以我一個人就搞定了。）

6. pick up 「取；拿」

↳ Have you picked up your plane tickets at the travel agent yet?（你到旅行社取回你的機票了嗎?）

7. on one's way 「在途中」

↳ Will you mail this package on your way to work?

（你可以在上班的途中寄這個包裹嗎?）

8. kick in 「開始生效」

↳ I feel the sleeping pills kicking in.

（我感覺到安眠藥開始生效了。）

9. get ～ through 「使～通過；完成」

↳ They failed to get the bill through Congress.

（他們無法在國會中讓這項法案通過。）

10. get over to 「去到」

↳ Let's get over to the front desk to pick up the message.

（我們一起走到櫃臺把留言取回吧。）

實力測驗

和你同期進公司的 A 先生是個內向樸實的人，最近卻聽說 A 先生要辭
去公司的工作自行創業。請試著以三種不同的說法表達你聽到這件事
情時的驚訝。

參考解答

1. That's very surprising!
2. How very surprising!
3. I find it incredible.

Halloween　　萬聖夜

Listening

Warm-up / Pre-questions

 請聽《Track 49》的新聞快報後回答下面問題。

下列哪一項說明符合新聞快報的內容？
  (A) 飯店將為孩子們舉辦萬聖夜狂歡晚會
  (B) 市中心的飯店因為萬聖夜狂歡的客人而熱鬧非凡
  (C) 五個主要飯店所有萬聖夜狂歡晚會的門票都已銷售一空

內容　Halloween is not just for kids anymore. All five of the major hotels downtown have sold out of their Halloween Bash tickets.

中譯　過萬聖夜不再是小孩子們的專利了。市區中五個主要大飯店所舉行的萬聖夜狂歡晚會門票皆已銷售一空。

解答　(C)

解說　Halloween 是萬聖節 (All Saints' Day) 的前夕（10 月 31 日晚上），為 All Hallows' Eve（萬聖之夜）的縮略語。在美國，其慶祝活動非常盛行，大家會把南瓜的中間挖空，做成南瓜燈籠 (jack-o'-lantern)，而裝扮成巫婆 (witch) 等妖魔鬼怪的小孩子會到鄰近地區挨家挨戶地敲門，並說 "Trick or treat!"（不給糖就搗蛋），藉此要到糖果。

kid 是較為口語的用法，在日常會話中比 child 更常使用。sell out of 為表示商店或人將貨物「全部銷售一空」的片語，用法如 We have completely sold out of the tickets.（票已完全售罄），以 we 等表示商店的詞語當作主詞。若把「販售的物品」當作主詞的話，

則可說成 The tickets sold out. 或是 The tickets are completely sold out.，而不需要加上 of。major 為「主要的」，bash 為口語用法，表示「晚會，派對」的意思。

Listening Step 1

 請聽《Track 50》的會話後回答下面問題。

Stephanie 拜託朋友 Joyce 什麼事？

(A) 幫忙看小孩

(B) 希望能借用化裝舞會的服裝

(C) 希望能一起分擔萬聖夜狂歡晚會的門票費用

解答 (A)

Listening Step 2

熟悉下列關鍵字

training program　訓練課程

break　休息，休假

fun　有趣的，好玩的

ticket　（門）票，入場券

babysitter　臨時保母

watch　照顧，看管

guilty　有罪惡感的，內疚的

trick-or-treating　萬聖夜的傳統，小孩子會到鄰近地區挨家挨戶地要糖果，並說 "Trick or treat!"（不給糖就搗蛋）。

supposed　應該

rush　趕；催促

serious 當真的，認真的
worth 值得
owe （義務上、道義上）虧欠

② 請聽《Track 51》並在括弧內填入正確答案。

1. Our (　　　　) just canceled out on us.
2. I would feel (　　) if I don't take the children trick-or-treating.
3. The babysitter was (　　　　) to do that while we were at the Halloween Bash.
4. Your kids can sleep over tomorrow night as well so you don't have to (　　　).
5. It'll be (　　　) it to be able to go.

解答

1. Our (babysitter) just canceled out on us.
2. I would feel (guilty) if I don't take the children trick-or-treating.
3. The babysitter was (supposed) to do that while we were at the Halloween Bash.
4. Your kids can sleep over tomorrow night as well so you don't have to (rush).
5. It'll be (worth) it to be able to go.

② 請再聽一次《Track 50》的會話後回答下面問題。

1. Bill 和 Stephanie 預定參加哪裡的萬聖夜狂歡晚會？
   (A) 孩子們的學校舉辦的萬聖夜狂歡晚會
   (B) 朋友 Joyce 家舉行的萬聖夜狂歡晚會

(C) 在飯店舉行的萬聖夜狂歡晚會

2. Stephanie 什麼時候會去接小孩?

(A) 星期五

(B) 星期六

(C) 星期日

解答   1. (C)　2. (B)

Listening Step 3

熟悉下列語句

hear from　接到～的來信或電話

put in　投入（勞力），花費（時間）

take a break　休假，休息

cancel out on　取消和～的約定

sell out　賣完

plan for a night out　計畫一個晚上的外出

sleep over　（在別人家）過夜

It's all set.　問題都解決了。

drop off　使下車

get off of work　下班

pick up　（開車）接

I owe you one.　我欠你一份人情。（感謝對方幫忙時的用語）

② 請聽《Track 52》並在括弧內填入正確答案。

1. You need to (　　) (　　) (　　) and do something fun.

2. Didn't that Bash (　　) (　　) a long time ago?

3. Just (   ) the kids (   ) tomorrow after you get off of work.

4. You can (   ) (   ) (   ) on Saturday whenever you and Bill get up.

5. Thanks again, Joyce. I (   ) (   ) (   ).

解答

1. You need to (take) a (break) and do something fun.

2. Didn't that Bash (sell) (out) a long time ago?

3. Just (drop) the kids (off) tomorrow after you get off of work.

4. You can (pick) (them) (up) on Saturday whenever you and Bill get up.

5. Thanks again, Joyce. I (owe) (you) (one).

② 請再聽一次《Track 50》的會話後回答下面問題。

1. Bill 和 Stephanie 為什麼會有萬聖夜狂歡晚會的門票?
   (A) 朋友送的
   (B) 趕在銷售一空之前買到的
   (C) 參加抽獎抽到的

2. Stephanie 的小孩將和誰一起去玩 "trick-or-treating"?
   (A) 和學校的朋友一起
   (B) 和 Joyce 的孩子一起
   (C) 和飯店的客人一起

3. Joyce 為何提議讓 Stephanie 的小孩在她家住一晚?
   (A) 因為萬聖節前夕的慶祝活動持續到半夜
   (B) 因為 Joyce 的孩子隔天還想跟他們玩
   (C) 因為這樣 Bill 和 Stephanie 就不用急著趕來接小孩

解答   1. (B)   2. (B)   3. (C)

Speaking

會話

 請再聽一次《Track 50》。

Stephanie: Hi, Joyce. How are you doing?

Joyce: Stephanie, it's great to hear from you. I'm fine. How have you been?

Stephanie: Incredibly busy! I've been putting in 10-hour days for over a month now, trying to get this new training program set up.

Joyce: I think you are working too hard, Stephanie. You need to take a break and do something fun.

Stephanie: Well, Joyce, Bill and I have tickets to go to the Halloween Bash at the Hilton Hotel downtown tomorrow night, but our babysitter just canceled out on us and I have no one to watch the kids.

Joyce: Didn't that Bash sell out a long time ago?

Stephanie: Yes, it did. We bought the tickets last month planning for this night out, but I would feel guilty if I don't take the children trick-or-treating. The babysitter was supposed to do that while we were at the Halloween Bash.

Joyce: Well, Stephanie, if you don't mind driving them out to my house I'll take them trick-or-treating with my kids while you and Bill go to the party. Your kids can sleep over tomorrow night as well so you don't have to rush.

Stephanie: Are you serious, Joyce?

Joyce: Of course I am. I'd be happy to help you out. You do need a break. You'll just have to drive an hour to get here.

Stephanie: That's so kind of you, Joyce. You are a real friend. I don't mind the drive at all. It'll be worth it to be able to go.

Joyce: Good then. It's all set. Just drop the kids off tomorrow after you get off of work and then you can pick them up Saturday whenever you and Bill get up.

Stephanie: That sounds great. Thanks again, Joyce. I owe you one.

中　譯 ....

史蒂芬妮： 嗨，喬伊絲，妳好嗎？

喬 伊 絲： 史蒂芬妮，真高興妳打電話來，我很好。妳呢？近來好嗎？

史蒂芬妮： 忙死了！為了讓新的訓練課程上軌道，我已經超過一個月每天上班十小時了。

喬 伊 絲： 妳真是工作過度了，史蒂芬妮，妳應該去度個假好好玩玩。

史蒂芬妮： 唉，喬伊絲，我和比爾有明晚在市中心希爾頓飯店所舉行的萬聖夜狂歡晚會門票，但是不巧我們的保母臨時取消，這下子沒人替我們看小孩啦！

喬 伊 絲： 狂歡晚會的門票不是早就銷售一空了嗎？

史蒂芬妮： 是啊，的確。我和比爾為了明晚的計畫，上個月就買好了門票。保母原來應該在我們參加狂歡晚會的同時帶孩子們去玩「不給糖就搗蛋」的遊戲，不過現在假

如我不帶他們去的話，我會非常內疚的。

喬伊絲：喔，史蒂芬妮，妳和比爾還是可以去參加狂歡晚會，假如妳不介意把孩子們送到我這兒來的話。我可以帶他們和我自己的孩子一起去玩「不給糖就搗蛋」。而且明晚他們可以留在我家過夜，這樣你們也不必趕來接他們了。

史蒂芬妮：喬伊絲，妳是當真的嗎？

喬伊絲：當然是啊。妳的確該放鬆一下了，我很樂意幫忙。妳只是需要開一小時的車到這裡來。

史蒂芬妮：喬伊絲，妳實在太好心了。妳真是我的好朋友。開車過去一點也不算什麼。只要能去參加狂歡晚會，一切都值得。

喬伊絲：那就好了。所有的問題都解決啦。妳只要在明天下班後把孩子送到這來，星期六等妳和比爾都睡飽了再過來接他們就好。

史蒂芬妮：真是個好主意。喬伊絲，多謝了，算我欠妳一次囉！

語 法

● hear from 與 hear of

hear from 這個詞語可用於書信、電話、留言。用法如：*Have* you *heard from* Tom lately?（最近湯姆有沒有捎信來？）/ It's great to *hear from* you.（很高興接到你的電話）/ I look forward to *hearing from* you.（我盼望收到你的信）。若要表示聽聞過某件事或某個人時，則用 hear of，其用法如：I've *heard of* her.（我聽說過她的事）/ I've never *heard of* her.（我從沒聽說過她）。

● while 與 during

雖然 while 與 during 在中文裡都是譯作「在～的期間」，但其實兩者

在用法上有極大的不同。while 是連接詞，所以它之後會接續從屬子句。相對地，during 則是介系詞，後面要接名詞、代名詞，或是相當於名詞、代名詞詞性的語句。舉例來說：while 的情況下要說成 I visited many museums *while* I was in New York. (停留在紐約的期間我拜訪了許多美術館)，during 的情況下則要說成 I visited many museums *during* my vacation in New York. (我在紐約度假時，拜訪了許多美術館)。此外，while 的子句中大多使用進行式，例如：He arrived *while* I was cooking dinner. (他到達時我正在做飯)，但像 Let's talk *while* we work out. (讓我們邊練習邊談談吧) 這樣的用法也很常見。

● whenever, wherever, however 等連接詞

在 when, where, how 等字之後加上 ever，就成了 whenever, wherever, however，其語意分別是「無論何時」、「無論何地」及「無論如何」。用法如 You can call me *whenever* you like. (你隨時可以打電話給我)/ The dog follows me *wherever* I go. (這隻狗一路跟著我) / You can do it *however* you like. (你可以用任何你喜歡的方式做)。

Speaking Function 15

「我很樂意為你做～（但條件是～）」「我不想～」

 請聽《Track 53》。

1. A: I'd be happy to take care of your kids.

   B: That's so kind of you.

2. A: I wonder if you're willing to exchange your room with another guest.

   B: Certainly, as long as the room is as good as my present one.

3. A: Do you mind babysitting my kids this Friday evening?

   B: I don't really want to babysit on Friday evening.

解說

● 要表示「我很樂意為你做～」，可以用 I'd be happy to ～來表達，to 的後面接續動詞的原形。例如「我很樂意幫你」就是 I'd be happy to help you.。happy 也可以用 most pleased 或 most delighted 來替換，改為 I'd be most pleased/delighted to help you.，句中的 most 用來強調語意。此外，也可以用 willing 或 prepared，說成 I'm quite willing/prepared to help you.。

● 「附帶有條件才願意幫忙做～」的情況下，可以在 Certainly 或 Yes, of course 之後加上 as long as / if / provided that / on the condition that / on the understanding that 等說法用以表示條件。比如說對於前來商借筆記型電腦的朋友，叮嚀他要小心使用時，可以說 Certainly, as long as you take good care of it.。

● 「並不願意幫忙做～」的情況下，又沒有什麼好的回絕方式時，可以用 I don't really want to ～ 的說法。不想借錢給人時就說 I don't really want to lend you any money.，或是 I don't think I can lend you any money.。若要使語氣和緩些，可以用 I'm not sure I can lend you any money. 的說法，相同的表達語句還有 I think I'd rather not to ～. 以及 I think I'd prefer not to ～.。

練習 1【代換】

② 請隨《Track 54》做代換練習。

1. *I'd be happy to*   take your kids trick-or-treating.

    I'd be most pleased to
    I'd be most delighted to
    I'm quite willing to
    I'm quite prepared to

2. "May I borrow your digital camera?"

"*Certainly, as long as*　　　　　you take good care of it."

"Certainly, if
"Certainly, provided that
"Certainly, on the condition that
"Certainly, with the understanding that

3. "Could you lend me some money?"

"*I don't really want to*　lend you any money."

"I don't think I can
"I'm not sure I can
"I think I'd rather not
"I think I'd prefer not to

練習 2【角色扮演】

 請隨《Track 55》在嗶一聲後唸出灰色部分的句子。

1. A: I'd be happy to drive you to the airport.
   B: That's so kind of you.

2. A: May I borrow this book?
   B: Certainly, as long as you return it by next Wednesday.

3. A: Could I use your car?
   B: I really don't want to let anybody use my car.

練習 3【覆誦重要語句】

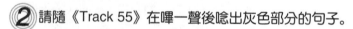 請隨《Track 56》覆誦英文句子。

1. take a break　「休假，休息」

↳What do you say we take a ten minute break?

（讓我們休息十分鐘好嗎?）

2. cancel out on 「取消和～的約定」

↳Betty was going to babysit our kids this evening, but she canceled out on us.

（貝蒂原本今晚要替我們看孩子的，不過她臨時取消了。）

3. sell out 「賣完」

↳I'm sorry, but tonight's show was completely sold out.

（很抱歉，今晚表演的門票已經賣完了。）

4. feel guilty 「有罪惡感，感到內疚」

↳I would feel guilty if I don't take my kids to the amusement park.

（假如我不帶孩子們去遊樂園玩，我會感到很內疚。）

5. supposed 「應該」

↳She was supposed to give me a call from the airport.

（她本來應該在機場打通電話給我的。）

6. sleep over 「（在別人家）過夜」

↳You've had too much to drink. Sleep over tonight.

（你已經喝太多，不能再喝了。今晚就在我家過夜吧。）

7. worth 「值得」

↳Learning how to use a spreadsheet is difficult, but it's worth it.

（學習如何用電腦表格計算雖然很難，但是很值得。）

8. drop off 「使下車」

↳Will you drop me off at that corner?

（請在那個街角讓我下車好嗎?）

9. get off of work 「下班」

  ↳ What time will you get off of work tomorrow?

  （你明天幾點下班？）

10. pick up 「（開車）接」

  ↳ I'll pick you up at your apartment at 8 o'clock.

  （八點鐘我來你家接你。）

實力測驗

你非常喜歡衝浪，並且是箇中好手。公司的某位同事最近開始迷上衝浪，拜託你教他衝浪的技巧。你當然是很乾脆地答應他囉！請試著以三種不同的說法告訴他你很樂意教他。

參考解答
　　　　　　1. I'd be happy to teach you how to surf.
　　　　　　2. I'd be most pleased to teach you how to surf.
　　　　　　3. I'd be most delighted to teach you how to surf.

輕鬆高爾夫英語

Marsha Krakower 著／劉明綱 譯

你因為英語會話能力不佳，到海外出差或旅行時，不敢與老外在高爾夫球場上一較高下嗎？本書忠實呈現了高爾夫球場上各種英語對話的原貌，讓你在第一次與老外打球時，便能應對自如！而即使不打高爾夫球的人，也可以從此書得到莫大的收穫，能對高爾夫文化有更深一層的了解。

同步口譯教你聽英語

斎藤なが子 著／劉明綱 譯

到底有沒有什麼方法可以增強英語聽力呢？──答案當然有。

本書為日本一位名同步口譯者的力作，書中提到許多正確聆聽及理解英語的聽力技巧，不僅對日本讀者受用，對於有心精進英語聽力的國內讀者而言，也一樣受益無窮。文中並且穿插許多作者多年來從事口譯心得的小單元，有志走上口譯之路的人務必一賭為快。

動態英語文法

阿部一 著 ／ 張慧敏 譯

翻開市面上的英語文法書，可以發現大部分都是文法規則說明，繁而雜的文法概念、生硬的解說，真是令人望而生怯，難道文法只能用這種方式學習嗎？請你不妨打開本書看看，作者是以談天的方式，生動地為你解說看似枯燥無味的文法概念，扭轉文法只能死背的印象，讓人驚訝文法竟然也能這麼有趣。

英語大考驗

小倉弘 著 ／ 本局編輯部 譯

想知道你的文法基礎夠紮實嗎？你以為所有的文法概念，老師在課堂上都會講到嗎？本書由日本補教界名師所執筆撰寫，將提供你一個思考英語的新觀點：學習英語文法，貴在理解，而非死背。藉由本書，重新審視之前所學的文法，將會發現：所有原本以為懂的、不懂的，或一知半解的問題，都可以在這本書裡找到答案！

社交英文書信

Janusz Buda、長野格、城戶保男 著 / 羅慧娟 譯

欣聞友人獲獎，你會用英文書寫恭賀信函嗎？商務貿易關係若僅止於格式化的書信往返，彼此將永遠不會有深層的互動。若想進一步打好人際關係，除了訂單、出貨之外，噓寒問暖也是必須的。本書特別針對商業人士社交上的需求而編寫，內容包羅萬象，是你最佳的社交英文書信指南。

商用英文書信

高崎榮一郎、Paul Bissonnette 著
篠田義明 監修 / 彭士晃 譯

閑熟商業用語、精通文法句型，寫起商務英文書信來就能得心應手嗎？其實商務書信的寫作就如同作文一般，起承轉合的拿捏才是關鍵。本書從商場實務的溝通原則出發，收集商業人士的實際範例，剖析英文書信的段落架構，追求清楚的內容邏輯，更列出改善範例以供對照，是一本從事貿易工作者最佳的商用英文書信指南。

透析商業英語的語法與語感

長野格 著 / 林山 譯

市面上講商業英語的書不少，但很少有一本書是專門針對商業英語語彙作解析。調查顯示，最令外語學習者感到挫折的往往不是有形的文法規則，而是難以捉摸的語感。畢竟商業英語不只是F.O.B.等基本商業知識，掌握熟悉字彙中的微妙語感與語法，才是縱橫商場的不二法門，也才能成為名副其實的洽商高手。

打開話匣子──Small Talk一下！

L. J. Link、Nozawa Ai 著 / 何信彰 譯

雙CD

你能夠隨時用英語與人Small Talk、閒聊一番嗎？有些人在正式的商業英語溝通上儘管應對自如，但是一碰到閒話家常，卻常常手足無措。本書即針對此問題，教你從找話題到接話題的秘訣。對話臨場感十足並語帶詼諧的本書，必定讓你打開話匣子，輕鬆講英文！

國家圖書館出版品預行編目資料

英語聽&說:中級篇 / 白野伊津夫, Lisa A. Stefani著;
沈薇譯.－－初版一刷.－－臺北市;三民,2003
面; 公分

ISBN 957-14-3852-9 (精裝)

1.英國語言－讀本

805.18   92009330

網路書店位址　http://www.sanmin.com.tw

© 英語聽&說
　　——中級篇

著作人　白野伊津夫　Lisa A. Stefani
譯　者　沈　薇
發行人　劉振強
著作財　三民書局股份有限公司
產權人　臺北市復興北路386號
發行所　三民書局股份有限公司
　　　　地址／臺北市復興北路386號
　　　　電話／(02)25006600
　　　　郵撥／00099985
印刷所　三民書局股份有限公司
門市部　復北店／臺北市復興北路386號
　　　　重南店／臺北市重慶南路一段61號
初版一刷　2003年6月
編　號　S 80441－1
基本定價　伍元捌角
行政院新聞局登記證局版臺業字第○二○○號

有著作權·不准侵害

ISBN 957-14-3852-9 (精裝)

白野伊津夫

日本明海大學副教授、明治大學講師。美國維吉尼亞大學口語傳播（Speech Communication）研究所碩士。著有多本與英語學習相關的書籍。

Lisa A. Stefani

美國加州 Grossmont College 講師。聖地牙哥州立大學碩士。亦有多本英語學習的相關著作問世。